WHITE WATER TRAIL

WHITE WATER TRAIL

A Western Trio

Dan Cushman

SAGEBRUSH
Large Print Westerns

First published in Great Britain by ISIS Publishing Ltd.
First published in the United States by Five Star

Published in Large Print 2008 by ISIS Publishing Ltd.,
7 Centremead, Osney Mead, Oxford OX2 0ES
United Kingdom
by arrangement with
Golden West Literary Agency

British Library Cataloguing in Publication Data
Cushman, Dan
White water trail: a western trio. – Large print ed. –
(Sagebrush western series)
1. Western stories
2. Large type books
I. Title II. Cushman, Dan. Phantom herds of Furnace
Flat III. Cushman, Dan. Boothill loves a pilgrim
813.5'4 [F]

ISBN 978–0–7531–8019–8 (hb)

Printed and bound in Great Britain by
T. J. International Ltd., Padstow, Cornwall

Table of Contents

The Phantom Herds of Furnace Flat

CHAPTER
ONE

The prairie that fronted the Windy Ridge Mountains was usually dusty white from baked alkali, but today it had a dark, vitreous cast after two days of rain. A miserable, cold drizzle. Long ago it had turned the stage road into a seething quagmire, well-nigh bottomless. As a result the stage was late. It was mid-afternoon when it came lurching up the rise from Bowstring Flats with Hoss Rogers, sodden and resigned, sitting in his lofty seat, alone. Hoss alternately cursed the rain, a pipe that would not stay lit, and the tinhorn gambler who had taken away forty-two of his slowly accumulated dollars playing three-card monte back in Split Rock the night before.

A front wheel dropped unexpectedly into a deep, water-filled hole. The coach lurched dangerously. Hoss cursed with a little extra venom and rolled out his long lash.

Inside, this sudden lurch had propelled Dusty Sears into the lap of his partner who sat opposite.

"Thanks for catchin' me, Yakima," Dusty said.

Yakima smoothed out his newspaper as though it were a valuable first edition of an ancient poet. This done, he made his habitual movement of removing his

3

Stetson and running his palm across the six strands of red hair that saved his dome from complete baldness.

"Still worryin' about that murder item?" Dusty asked.

"Yep!"

"Just a killin'." Dusty was tall, and young, and easygoing. He didn't borrow trouble. "There's always likely to be a killin'."

Dusty tried to stretch his legs to a more comfortable position, but in this he was hampered by the tall cowboy who was snoring beside Yakima.

"Sure, there'll always be killin's," Yakima agreed, "but this here ain't just an ordinary one. I wouldn't be surprised if it had somethin' to do with this trip of ours. Here, squint at this news item."

Dusty had read the item when he bought the paper back in Split Rock, but he read it again anyhow.

ANOTHER KILLING

Cyrus Woolridge was found dead on his north range last week. He had been shot in the back. Sheriff Till of Watson County and two of his deputies are now riding out to investigate.

This is the second mysterious killing in the Wagonhammer district so far this month, and the Editor of the Gazette is going to be so bold as to wonder what is wrong in our neighboring community around Dry River that an honest rancher like Cy isn't safe from

rustlers and dry-gulchers when he's right in the shadow of his own corral.

Cyrus Woolridge was born about 1836 in Missouri and came West on a Missouri River steamboat in . . .

Dusty scanned Woolridge's obituary, then he read once more through the account of his death. "They're always feuding in that Wagonhammer country," he remarked.

The lanky cowboy suddenly stopped snoring and lifted one eyelid. "Old Cy never feuded with nobody," he said. With that, the eye went shut again and the heavy breathing continued.

"He didn't?" Dusty asked.

"No, sir! Old Cy was right peaceful." This time the lanky one roused sufficiently to open both eyes. "Better-hearted fellow you wouldn't be able to find if you traveled Montana Territory from end to end. He had a little ranch on Spring Creek . . . that's a tributary to the Wagonhammer. Nothing much . . . run three or four hundred head of Texas cattle. Once a year he rode to Dry River and took on a load of tangle-foot, but he never had an enemy in the world."

"He must have had one enemy," Dusty stated.

"Not necessarily. I have an idee old Cy was dry-gulched because he happened to find out somethin' he shouldn't."

Dusty was thoughtful. Like Yakima, he had a pretty strong suspicion that this killing was somehow wound up with the very thing that was taking them to the Wagonhammer. There was something sinister about it

5

all. It had seemed that way to Dusty right from the first. It was not a feud — it was some well-laid plot.

Dusty carefully balanced himself against the vehicle's unpredictable lurching while he sprinkled tobacco into a wheat-straw paper and twisted it into shape. He lit it, and squinted through the smoke at the lank cowpuncher. "What is going on up there?"

The lanky one sat for a while without answering. Then, in a slow, significant voice: "Stranger, I'm just a peaceful forty-a-month 'puncher. I don't very frequent stick my nose into the other man's corral. There's been lots of lead flyin' around the Wagonhammer of late, and I suppose one reason none of it ever connected with me is because I always minded my own business." He looked beyond Dusty at the dripping landscape that crept past the window. "Rainy weather we have been havin', ain't it?" he asked.

Dusty mutely agreed.

The coach rolled on. After a time, Yakima slept. The lanky cowboy resumed his snoring. Dusty fingered the newspaper thoughtfully. His mind went back to one day a week before.

He had been called to the territorial capital for an interview with the Old Man. The Old Man, in this case, was T. H. Hawley, owner of the Lazy J spread where Dusty had been foreman for the last three years. He also owned this other ranch — the Circle 2 on the Wagonhammer. On his arrival, Dusty had been shown to a huge, ornate drawing room. Plush furniture with tassels. Dusty was nervous. He twisted his Stetson in a tight roll while he waited for the Old Man to say something.

"Hello, Dusty," the Old Man said.

"Hello, T.H.," he answered.

They shook hands. The Old Man's palm was hot, his skin was dry like old paper, but the muscles beneath were strong as harness leather.

"Have a cigar?" he asked.

"No, thanks." Dusty instantly wondered whether he should have taken the cigar. He felt self-conscious. "I always roll 'em," he explained, shifting to the other foot.

"Sure," said the Old Man, "so do I."

The Old Man thereupon pulled from his coat pocket a sack of tobacco and papers. They each rolled one. For some reason, sight of the Old Man, rolling that cigarette, took all the nervousness out of Dusty.

They had a long talk. When he left the mansion, Dusty still wasn't sure about the job on which he was being sent. He wasn't sure because the Old Man himself wasn't sure. But this was it, at least on the surface — he was being sent to the Circle 2 as foreman under the ranch manager, Rex Benton.

"There's some things up there that just ain't according to the book," the Old Man had said. "Every year we lose more cows in snowdrifts than any other outfit. Every year the rustlers run more brands on us. We never get our share of slicks. Every year we lose too much money. I'm not saying it's Benton. In fact, I'm sure it ain't. Benton

7

is honest. But there's some funny things goin' on up there I expect you to track down. And one word of advice. Don't trust anybody. That is . . . nobody except one. That one is Jim Brant. Jim and I trailed up to the country when it was still owned by the Blackfeet. You can trust Brant. If you get in a tight spot, go to him. But aside from him, don't get confidential with anybody." The Old Man had smiled and pulled out his makings. "Maybe not even with me."

Dusty thought back over this while he looked out at the sodden prairie. Yes, there was something funny going on in the Wagonhammer country. Mighty funny.

The coach joggled across the prairie for time that seemed interminable. Then, with a scraping of muddy brake shoes, it tilted forward down a steep grade. This unexpected change in equilibrium caused Yakima to rouse and look from the window.

"Coulée," he said.

The road hung dangerously to the coulée's cutbank side for the first 300 feet of the descent, then the grade became gentler and the coach rolled safely across the level ground at the bottom. The horses went splashing across a rain-fed stream, then the road wound through a grove of cottonwood and box elder trees. Emerging, a long log building and some corrals came in sight.

Hoss Rogers pulled his team to a stop in front of the building, climbed down stiffly from his high seat, flung open the coach's door.

"Roll out and stretch your legs!" he shouted. "This is Bedrock station. It's a long drag yet to Dry River. Can't tell, maybe old Ike has a pot of beans a-cookin'."

They got out on cramped legs. Immediately their boots sank into the gumbo ooze. Yakima started to swear, stopped abruptly. His jaw sagged. Quickly recovering himself, he swept off his hat and made a motion at brushing down his six red hairs. He was looking at the door. Dusty looked, too.

Standing there was the most beautiful girl he had ever seen. She was a girl one might expect on a calendar picture, or maybe in surroundings like the Old Man's drawing room at the territorial capital, but here, in the door of this dingy stage station . . . Dusty closed his eyes tightly and looked again. She was still there.

Her hair was drawn up mannishly and tucked under a broad, brown sombrero. She wore a simple brown blouse and riding skirt. From beneath the riding skirt one neat boot toe protruded. Dusty realized she was looking at him. He took off his hat. Apparently unconscious of the surprise she had created, the girl turned to the driver.

"Hello, Hoss," she said. "I thought you'd never make it."

Hoss grinned. "Miss Leona, if I'd known you was waitin', there'd be lather on them broncos' hides so thick they could have shaved. But what the thunder are you doin' here at Bedrock?"

"I took the short cut to town and my horse went lame. I hope you have room for me."

Yakima stepped forward and bowed gallantly, the raindrops spattering, unheeded, on his scalp. "You can have my seat," he offered.

Hoss looked at him witheringly. "She can have the hull interior if she wants it, and you cowpokes can ride aback in the boot."

She laughed. "I'm sure there's no need of that."

Dusty felt awkward, standing there, not saying anything. He shifted from one long leg to the other. He noticed she was looking at him again. Perhaps he should say something. Nothing suitable came to mind. Then she turned and went back inside.

A grizzled man wearing buckskin trousers and the dirtiest shirt in Dusty's recollection appeared from the corral leading a team of horses, and a half-breed boy followed him with two more. The grizzled man proved to be Ike, master of Bedrock station. After hitching six fresh horses and turning the mud-spattered beasts into the corral, he tilted his face toward the sky and called in a sing-song voice: "They's beans in the pot, an' biscuits in the pan. All baked and brown and fitten for a man." On completion of his homespun rhyme, he burst into a raucous laugh and slapped his buckskin pant leg. Ike never tired of laughing, even though he had repeated the same words to each incoming coach for the last five years.

Dusty was hungry, but one look at Ike's reeking shirt was enough to make him hesitate. He didn't notice that the girl had returned to the door and was watching him.

"I ain't 'special hungry," he said. "I ate pretty big in Split Rock."

Ike's eyelids drooped balefully. "There's a stout cottonwood limb and a lariat cravat waitin' for the cowboy which turns down these biscuits, stranger. These was baked by Miss Leona yonder." Dusty no longer hesitated.

A minute later they had gathered at Ike's rough plank table. The biscuits were brown and delicious. There were also baked beans and crisp salt pork.

After a mouthful or two, Yakima turned to Leona. "I hope your hoss ain't lamed bad."

"Bad enough, I'm afraid. He lost a shoe," she answered.

Yakima's headshake expressed great sorrow. "Have you rode far?"

"Just from the ranch. We live out on the Wagonhammer."

At mention of the Wagonhammer, Dusty glanced at her sharply. She looked at him questioningly. He explained: "We've been reading about the trouble there."

He expected her to make some answer, but she remained silent, devoting her attention to her plate of salt pork and beans.

CHAPTER
TWO

The meal was finished. The six fresh horses easily took the coach up the steep road that led from the coulée. Leona, sitting across from Dusty, was still preoccupied. The coach cleared the brow and rolled across the level prairie. A breeze swept from the east carrying through the glassless windows a few cold spatters of rain.

Unexpectedly she said: "The trouble on the Wagonhammer . . . you mean those killings?"

Dusty explained: "We're headed there ourselves. I'm Dusty Sears, new foreman of the Circle Two, and this is Yakima, my top hand."

An expression of pleasure lit the girl's face. "Why, we're neighbors! I'm Leona Brant. Our ranch is about eight miles south of the Circle Two."

"You're not *Jim* Brant's daughter?"

"Yes, do you know him?"

"No. Only by word of mouth. You see, the Old Man . . . my boss, T. H. Hawley . . ."

"He's an old friend of Dad's."

"I know. He wants me to call on your father as soon as I get there."

This wasn't exactly the truth. The Old Man hadn't told him to call. All he'd said was that Jim Brant could be trusted, but Dusty didn't bother to go into all that.

Leona said: "I'm going out to the ranch tomorrow, or the day after, as soon as I take care of some business at the bank. That is, I'll go to the ranch provided I can borrow a horse in town."

"We'll drive you out," Yakima horned in with a flourish. "Rex Benton, manager of the Circle Two, is sending in a buckboard for us."

Leona started to thank Yakima, but she stopped abruptly. The coach came to a sudden halt. The unexpectedness of it almost threw her from the seat.

"What the thunder!" exclaimed Yakima. He looked from the window, jerked back. His hand instinctively went to his hip, but his six-gun was jammed between his body and the side of the coach.

An instant later the door was flung open from the outside.

"Keep your hands innocent, strangers."

A stern-looking man stood there covering them with two guns. "Climb down," he ordered.

He was square-faced, about forty. He didn't look like a road agent. He looked like some honest, hard-riding rancher. He had three companions, none of whom had bothered to dismount. They watched from a distance of five or six yards. Two of these were obviously ranchers like himself. The third had a hard and shifty face, a half- or quarter-breed. He carried two silver-mounted pistols with pearl handles, and across the pommel of his saddle he balanced a Winchester.

Leona started to climb down.

"You don't need to get down, Miss Leona," the first man said.

She resolutely came down anyway. "What's the meaning of this, Joel?" she demanded sharply. "Ranching must be getting to be poor when you take to stopping stages."

Joel answered: "Ranching's getting unhealthy, if that's what you mean."

"Oh, that trouble on the Wagonhammer! What has stopping this stage got to do with that?"

"Just this . . . there's too many varmints in the country already."

"Meaning you don't want us?" Dusty asked, indicating Yakima and himself.

"Exactly," Joel answered coldly. He paid no attention to the lanky cowboy.

"Maybe you don't know who we are. I'm Dusty Sears, new foreman of the Circle Two. This is Yakima, my top hand. Rex Benton is meeting us in Dry River. He'll vouch for us."

The men glanced at one another significantly. The half-breed with the pearl-handled revolvers laughed. It wasn't a pleasant laugh.

Joel answered: "You won't fool us with that story. We've been warned you were coming. Get your war bags, if you have any." He pointed back down the two streaks of wet that marked the road's wandering course through the prairie grasses. "See that trail? Take it. Take it and keep a-goin'. Dry River ain't healthy for your breed, and the Wagonhammer ain't, neither."

Leona came forward. Her voice flashed anger. "Joel! What's got into you? These men are all right. They're not gunmen. They're just what they say they are."

"Do you know 'em?" Joel asked.

"Certainly."

"Known 'em for long?"

Leona didn't answer.

"When'd you meet 'em?"

"At Bedrock station."

"Then *how* do you know they ain't gunmen?"

"I just do, that's all. Any blind person could see they aren't cattle rustlers, or gunmen, or whatever you take them to be."

"Miss Leona, if they're headed thataway" — he gestured down the trail — "why we won't need to worry whether they are or not. If your paw was here, he's say the same."

The half-breed spoke up in a sharp, nasal voice: "Better get those guns." Then, when Joel hesitated, he dismounted, strode over, snatched Dusty's six-shooter from the holster. He looked at it. The gun was an unusual make — a .41 caliber with an octagonal barrel.

Joel said: "No, Basette. Let them keep their guns. This ain't robbery. We'll be able to take care of them if they make a wrong move."

Basette reluctantly dropped the gun back in Dusty's holster.

Joel nodded to Leona and the lanky cowboy. "Better get back inside." He gestured to Hoss. "All right, get moving."

Dusty could feel Leona's eyes on him. He looked up at her face framed in the window. She seemed about to speak, but the coach started with a jerk. It rolled away, the horses splashing mud and water from the sodden road.

Joel watched the coach for a few seconds, then he turned and spoke: "All right, boys, get a-goin'. Don't get any fancy notions just because we're lettin' you keep your guns. It will be a rough trip back to Bedrock, but I imagine it will help you remember about this all the better."

Dusty was known for the slowness of his temper — for that almost as widely as for the reliability of his judgment of horseflesh and the unerring nature of his marksmanship. But his temper had now reached the ragged edge. He demanded: "What the damnation is the meaning of this?"

It was a tense moment. Basette's right hand caressed the butt of one pearl-handled revolver while his other cocked the hammer of the Winchester. He was like a rattler ready to uncoil.

Joel brought his gun barrels level. "Get goin'," he said.

It would have been suicide to resist. Dusty and Yakima started back along the trail. At every step their boots sank in the mud. They took to the prairie where footing was a little better. After a couple hundred yards they turned and looked back. The four men sat their horses, watching. The dull, rainy-day light reflected back brightly from the butts of Basette's pearl-handled guns.

Dusty and Yakima hunted out a deep clump of greasewood near the brow of Bedrock coulée and waited. They saw no more of Joel, Basette, and the two others. Hours passed.

"Guess they must have took us for somebody else," said Yakima.

"I doubt it. They seemed to know we were coming. I guess for some reason they ain't anxious to have a new foreman on the Circle Two."

"Something blamed funny goin' on in that Wagonhammer country."

About sundown the clouds broke away. The moon came up blue-white over the rambling low peaks of the Windy Ridge Mountains. The prairie, by moonlight, took on a crystalline appearance. The breeze was chilly like late fall.

"I'm hungry," moaned Yakima. "Let's go down to the station and eat some more of Ike's beans."

"Listen!"

There was a movement in the direction of the road where it climbed from the coulée. It was a regular, creaking noise. It grew steadily louder. Wagons.

"Probably a freighter," said Dusty.

"At this time of night? A freighter would put up at the station."

In a minute, two wagons, pulled by a long string of mules, appeared over the coulée's brow. They stepped forward.

"Ho, pardner!" Dusty signaled.

The driver made a movement of surprise.

"No need for that cannon," Dusty added.

The driver, somewhat reassured by the sound of Dusty's honest drawl, dropped the barrel of his six-shooter to a less dangerous angle and scrutinized the two men who approached him. He had pulled his ten-mule team to a stop; now he wrapped the lines around the tall hand brake.

"Who is it?" he asked.

"Couple of tired cowboys."

"And hungry," added Yakima.

"What in the name of Jerry-ko are you doin' up here?"

"Waitin' for a ride from a muleskinner."

The driver was somewhat reassured by the squinty old eyes. His gray-stubbled chin revolved slowly around a cud of tobacco. He dropped back his heavy Colt revolver, satisfied.

"Hop aboard," he invited. It was a long, tiresome trip to Dry River, especially at night. He was thankful for the company. "Tired and hungry cowboys are welcome on Milk River Jordan's outfit."

Dusty and Yakima climbed to the seat beside him. In a few seconds the long string was moving again. The wooden axles, wet and swollen, creaked dismally.

Dusty took time to look the outfit over. The loads appeared to consist of squarish wooden boxes, although he couldn't be sure as both wagons were carefully covered by large canvas drapes. He rolled a cigarette, felt for a match.

"Hold on!" Milk River Jordan grabbed his arm.

"What's wrong?"

"No smokin'."

"No?"

"Them's my words, cowboy. No smokin'." Milk River laid out his long rawhide lash and brought it to a stop with a report like a pistol shot a few inches above the rump of one lagging mule. He put back the lash and spurted a generous stream of tobacco juice at a clump of sagebrush off in the moonlight. He went on: "You see, we got religion here on this wagon, and I just found out that commandment number eleven reads . . . no smokin'. Smokin' is bad for the liver. It's a temptation of Satan. A pitfall."

Dusty grinned and tossed away his cigarette.

Milk River reached down among the roll of soogans under the seat. He pulled out a bottle. "Trade whiskey," he said. "Good for man or Cree. Let this warm your innards instead."

The whiskey was raw, but, as Milk River said, it warmed Dusty's innards. He passed it on to Yakima.

The outfit creaked on through the night. Dusty sat thinking. Funny, this no smoking deal. Milk River had about as much religion as a porcupine. But he meant what he said about no smoking.

"Heavy load?" said Yakima.

"Heavy," agreed Milk River.

Dusty looked around, wondering what was in those boxes under the tarps. Milk River, guessing his thought, said: "Four hundred and forty-four cases of blackjack eatin' tobacco for old Ezra Cibber. Dry River storekeeper and philanthropist, kindest-hearted man ever to beat a widda out of her inheritance."

19

Milk River volunteered no more information, and Dusty knew better than to ask for it. But all the same he intended to make the acquaintance of this Ezra Cibber as soon as he arrived in Dry River.

It was after midnight when the wagons creaked into town. Milk River turned down a side street, avoiding the line-up of saloons, gambling houses, and bird cages that, despite the lateness of the hour, still enjoyed good business. Somewhere a merrymaking fiddle sawed out "The Devil's Dream" and a more distant piano clashed discordantly. Someone let out an echoing: "*Yip-ee!*"

"Nice here in civilization, ain't it?" Milk River asked.

He pulled the mules to a stop. A few hundred feet distant was a two-story building with a warped false front. It was dark save for a light that burned in one small back window.

"Yonder is Ezra Cibber's store," he said. "Like me, Ezra is a powerful religious man. But he might not take kindly to passengers, even ones that don't smoke. So I'll just drop you boys here, and I'll thank you to let your means of locomotion remain secret."

After Milk River had pulled away, Dusty said: "There's a funny one."

"What is?"

"That load of his."

"Load of blackjack eatin' tobacco," Yakima stated confidently.

"Not in cases like that. And that no smoking rule . . ."

"He's religious. He said that smokin' was a pitfall of Satan."

"Yakima, I hope it won't spoil your appetite none to find out we been atop a wagonload of dynamite."

"Dynamite! What would a storekeeper want with two wagonloads of dynamite in a cow camp like this?"

"That," answered Dusty, "is something I aim to find out."

CHAPTER
THREE

Dry River had one hotel — **Mollie Skettle's Cowboy's Rest and Saloon**. They asked about accommodations, but all the beds were taken. They ended by sleeping in the loft of a livery stable.

Next morning, they inquired about the expected rig from the Circle 2. The Old Man had written to Rex Benton, telling him when they would arrive. The buckboard should have met yesterday's stage — but no one in Dry River had seen anyone from the Circle 2. Dusty was troubled. They ate breakfast and started back toward the livery barn. Its owner had a rig for hire.

"Is your name Dusty Sears?"

He turned at sound of his name. A young man was approaching. By his black sleeve protectors Dusty guessed he was a clerk.

"That's my name," Dusty answered.

"My boss wants to see you."

"Your boss?"

"Ezra Cibber . . . at the store."

Dusty recalled his resolve to see Cibber, and now here was the man sending for him. Marveling at the

22

nature of fate, he gestured for Yakima to follow and the three headed for Cibber's.

They entered. It was cool inside. It had a pungent odor, a mingling of tanned leather, smoked meats, and moldy burlap. They looked around. Cibber apparently had one of everything on hand, stacked in shelves, hanging from rafters, heaped in corners — sardines and anvils, sunbonnets and horse collars, brown sugar, whiskey, riding boots, and bullet molds.

A stooped, gray-haired man advanced toward them, walking almost silently although he wore hard-heeled riding shoes. He had on small steel-rimmed glasses around which his sharp eyes roved. Those eyes — they made Dusty uncomfortable. They were pale blue, bleached, and they had no kindness in them.

"Sears?" Cibber had a harsh, magpie voice. His quick eyes fell on Yakima. "Who's this?"

"This is Yakima, my pardner."

"Oh. Your partner. Glad to know you. Glad to know you both." Unexpectedly he laughed. His laugh sounded like a restaurant parrot's. "I suppose people have already told you I'm crazy?"

"Should they have?" asked Dusty.

Cibber's gimlet eyes bored into him, and from that moment they seemed to understand each other. "That remains to be seen," said Cibber. Then with one of the unexpected movements that were habitual with him: "My office is back there. I want to talk to you." When Yakima made a move to follow, he added: "Alone!"

Cibber's office contained just enough room for a battered table and two chairs.

"Sit down and be at home," Cibber said with an attempt at cordiality. He offered a cigar.

"No thanks, I'll roll one."

"I understand you're the new foreman at the Circle Two out on the Wagonhammer."

"That's correct."

"Dangerous place, the Wagonhammer country." He paused for effect. "Yes, sir, mightee dangerous. I hate to see a young man like you run into trouble, and your partner, what did you say his name was . . . ?"

"Yakima."

"Yes. Yakima. I'd hate to see him run into trouble, too. You know, there have been two men killed on that range in the last month. Shot down in cold blood." Cibber's pale eyes shifted around the steel rims of his glasses. "Horrible."

"So I'd suppose. Murder generally is."

"Um, yes. An unpleasant place to be foreman, I'd say offhand."

"What are you getting at, Cibber?"

"Just this. I'm putting on a large ranch promotion out on Furnace Flat. I need a foreman. A *good* foreman. And I have the money to pay. Work for me and I'll double the money you get at the Circle Two. Three hundred a month. Is that a deal?"

Dusty was not tempted. However, he wanted to hear Cibber out. He said: "That depends."

"On what?"

"Various things. Where is this Furnace Flat?"

"South of the mountains. Near the river breaks."

"Is there a ranch out there now?"

"Just a camp at Indian Wells."

Dusty had heard the Old Man speak of Furnace Flat. It was a bone-dry range occupying the broad, flat benches overlooking the Missouri River breaks. During the heat of July and August, cattle that were ranged on Furnace Flat would wander down through the wild breaks — the badlands — to water on the river, and once in that madly scrambled country no roundup crew ever got more than a fraction back. As a result the breaks became a mavericker's paradise, and every big cow outfit south of the Windy Ridge kept their herds turned from Furnace Flat.

Dusty pretended ignorance: "Plenty of water?"

Cibber scrunched in his chair uncomfortably. "Let me worry about the water. I'll pay your wages . . . every cent and on the day they're due. Twice as much as you're getting at the Circle Two. Is it a deal?"

Dusty got up. "I'm afraid not."

Cibber's hands clutched the edge of the table like the claws of some bird of prey. Then he pulled open a drawer, dug through a medley of papers, and drew out a heavy buckskin bag. His fingers fumbled with the drawstring. He opened it, dumped out a little heap of $20 and $10 gold pieces. Dusty estimated that about $1,000 lay in the pile.

"A little advance in salary," Cibber explained. "Maybe you would like to take a trip. It gets a little hot here later in the summer."

"No. I think I'll go on being foreman on the Circle Two. When I take a job, I like to finish it. Thanks for the offer, anyhow."

Cibber seemed to freeze with the words. He started picking up the gold pieces and dropping them, one by one, in the buckskin bag.

"By the way, Cibber, I'd like to buy a few sticks of dynamite. You don't happen to sell it, do you?"

For several seconds the only sound was that of coins clinking in the sack.

"Never handle it," Cibber answered.

"One thing I can't figure out," Dusty said to Yakima when they were on their way back to the livery barn, "is how he knew that three hundred dollars was exactly twice what I was getting at the Circle Two."

At the barn, the proprietor had proudly wheeled out the rig he kept for hire. It was a surrey with a fancy fringed canopy, polished mahogany side panels, and a great deal of expensive brass hardware. Lots of stables hired out common buckboards, and only a few had top buggies, but this stable possessed a surrey! The owner had fallen heir to it by accident — it had been the pride of a dude rancher who brought it with him to the country a few years before, then left it behind when a succession of scorching summers, howling winters, and the depredations of the Tucker gang of rustlers bankrupted him.

A hostler then led out two extremely snaky cayuse horses and tried to back them to the trees. They snorted and looked at the surrey with wild eyes, but finally, after some rough persuasion, they submitted to the traces, and stood, muscles twitching under their hides as if in warning that any unexpected sound or action would make them jump to kingdom come.

Yakima smoothed down his six red hairs and looked at the team dubiously.

Their owner said: "Just let 'em run for a mile or three to get the vinegar out of their veins and they'll be all right." Then he became stern and shook a warning finger. "But don't injure that surrey. You do and it'll cost you cowpokes a year's salary." He stopped suddenly and took off his hat. " 'Scuse me, Miss Leona, if I swore. I didn't see you come up."

Dusty and Yakima turned quickly around. Leona was standing there. She had come up so quietly they hadn't heard her. Today she didn't wear the riding skirt and brown blouse — she had discarded that rough attire for a frilly dress, many sizes too large. She was a trifle embarrassed about the dress.

She said: "It belongs to Kate Bosler. I stayed with the Boslers last night and Kate was good enough to lend it to me."

Dusty stumbled for words. What was the matter with him? Why did this girl make him feel so awkward? Other girls hadn't. While he stood there, trying to think of something to say, Yakima, that devil among the women, swept off his hat with a grandee's flourish, allowing the sun to reflect unhampered from his shiny dome. "You look beautiful!"

Leona smiled. "I never expected to see you two here in Dry River."

27

Dusty found his voice: "Shucks, it will take more'n your friends, Joel and Basette, to run us out of the country."

"Don't feel too hard toward Joel. He's really a good man. His name is Joel Sims. He has a ranch down the Wagonhammer. But Basette . . ." She made a wry face. "The other two, Rance and Jeffers, they're ranchers, too. I know they were wrong when they put you off the coach, but you can't blame them for trying to keep gunmen out of the country. Not after those killings."

"Sure."

She turned her attention to the gleaming, brass-trimmed surrey. "Don't tell me you've hired it."

"Yes, ma'am. Isn't she a beauty?" Dusty passed his hand admiringly over one of the mahogany panels.

"I was figuring on hiring it myself."

Yakima again leaped to the fore. "Won't you allow us to drive you?"

"I'd be pleased."

Dusty was pleased, too.

The surrey's wide, tasseled top spread over them like a caliph's canopy. They rode grandly, safe from the white-hot morning sun. The road's surface had dried quickly, and, before many miles had been covered, the slim wheels began kicking up a fine film of dust. It doesn't stay wet for long in the prairie country.

Ahead, they could see the road for miles, winding up the slowly rising benches like a white, uncoiled snake. After a few swift miles, the two cayuse horses worked the edge off their energy and proved to be a good team — small, but wiry and steady-going.

"How far is it to the Wagonhammer?" Dusty asked, knowing quite well how far it was.

"About twenty-five miles."

"I made the acquaintance of Mister Cibber this morning," he went on, still searching for a subject of conversation.

"Oh, Ezra Cibber?" She laughed. "He's crazy, isn't he?"

"I don't know whether he is or not."

"What I mean is that people consider him queer on lots of subjects. But he's always been smart in business matters . . . at least until lately."

"What's happened lately?"

"He's supposed to be bringing in a herd of pilgrim cattle from Iowa to stock the Furnace Flat range."

"Is that crazy?"

"I wouldn't call it very smart. Furnace Flat is a dry-bone range. When the water in Furnace Creek plays out along in July, all the riders in the territory couldn't keep cows from drifting down into the river breaks. And once they get in there, no roundup can ever hunt them out. There's some water at Indian Wells, but you could hoist night and day without getting enough for fifty head."

"Does Furnace Creek run from the south side of the mountains?"

"No, it headwaters right by the Wagonhammer. In fact, it *used to be* the Wagonhammer."

Dusty hid his interest by pretending to be dissatisfied with the pace of one of the cayuses. "What do you mean . . . used to be the Wagonhammer?" he asked, jerking at one line.

"It's like this . . . the Wagonhammer water comes mainly from the Big Sixty Springs back in the mountains. According to a geologist who was here one time, the water from the springs once flowed down the valley of Furnace Creek, across Furnace Flat, and to the river. There wasn't any such thing as the Wagonhammer. But a million or so years ago, during the Ice Age, a glacier came along and left a dam of dirt and gravel which caused the water to cut a new valley . . . the Wagonhammer."

"You mean it's just this dam of dirt and rocks that keeps the Wagonhammer running? Otherwise Furnace Creek and Furnace Flat would get all the water, and the Wagonhammer range would be bone dry?"

"I guess so."

Dusty was about to ask something else, but Yakima, who was sitting in the rear seat, leaned forward and tapped his shoulder. "Would it surprise you to know we was being followed?" He pointed back.

Dusty looked just in time to see three riders disappear into a coulée. He watched for them to reappear, but there was no more sign of them.

"Just travelin' like we are," Dusty said, but his voice lacked conviction.

"Them's coulée riders," Yakima warned, "and, if there's one thing I'm distrustful of more'n somethin' else, it's coulée riders."

They drove on. Dusty kept watch, but there was no further sign of the three horsemen. Two or three hours passed.

Far away, below, the white sunlight reflected from a little patch of shiny objects — the scattering frame buildings of Dry River. Ahead of them the road kept climbing the benches. As they neared the mountains, the land became more rolling. In one place it circled a rounded hill on whose crest protruded a heap of large, blackish boulders. It approached to within 100 yards of this natural fortification, then it cleared a shoulder of a knoll and could be seen looping down across a gentle saddle toward a coulée. It would have been easy for the riders to have reached the coulée farther down and then double back for an ambush. Dusty looked at the coulée suspiciously, but it was still four or five miles away.

A gun cracked. A bullet fanned the air under the surrey's canopy, plowed the earth forty or fifty yards distant, droned away like a bumblebee. More shots — the sharp reports of two .30-30s — the deeper sound of a Colt. Splinters showered from a mahogany panel.

With the sound of the first shot, almost as if he had anticipated it, Dusty had leaped to his feet and begun lashing the rumps of the startled cayuses with the loose ends of his reins. They bolted in a wild gallop. They deserted the road in favor of the open prairie. The surrey leaped and cavorted behind, every moment threatening to outspeed them.

Puffs of powder smoke drifted in the still air above the rocks at the hilltop. Undaunted by the surrey's careening flight, Yakima held fast with one hand, whipped out his .45, and emptied it in the direction of their attackers.

31

More shots. Leona half lost her grip on the seat. She jumped up and took hold of the frame of the vehicle. Her dress billowed in the breeze. Instantly the firing stopped.

In a few seconds they were beyond .30-30 range, but Dusty played safe and kept the horses at a good gallop for half a mile, and after that he pulled them down to a swift trot.

Yakima finished reloading his six-shooter. He patted it fondly. "Guess they cut off their fandango pretty sudden when Mabel here cut loose."

Dusty was doubtful. "I doubt it was Mabel."

Yakima looked hurt.

"I think it was more likely Leona than Mabel. Looked to me that shootin' stopped when Miss Leona's dress puffed out. Likely that was the first they knew we had a woman along. My guess is those dry-gulchers were afraid they'd have the whole country riled if they killed her . . . or maybe they were just chivalrous."

They kept watch on the rocks. After a while the riders appeared and rode swiftly away. It was too far to tell anything about them, except that two rode dark horses, and one a gray. Silvery gun shine reflected time and again from the body of the man on the gray horse.

Dusty kept the cayuses at a good pace all the way to the coulée. The road dropped steeply down; in the bottom it wound for a while among thick bullberry bushes and gnarled box elders, then it climbed to the bench on the other side. They all breathed easier when the coulée was behind them.

Leona said: "We're safe now. This is our range. Dad has a camp a mile or two away."

They reached the camp without incident.

There were two cowboys there. One of them caught and saddled a horse for Leona. She rode away. Just before she disappeared from sight over the crest of a knoll, she turned and waved.

Dusty jiggled the reins and clucked to the cayuse horses. "There goes the prettiest girl in the territory," he said sadly.

Yakima nodded agreement.

CHAPTER
FOUR

The Wagonhammer was a swift, clear stream, seldom more than ten or twelve feet wide. Its course through the low, sun-browned foothills was marked by a winding streak of green. The road followed the stream for several miles, crossing and re-crossing it. Then, at the far edge of some meadowland, they caught sight of the scattered log buildings of the Circle 2.

When the surrey rolled up, there was no sign of life, save for three horses that stood in one of the corrals leisurely switching flies.

"Whoa," said Dusty. He wrapped the reins around the brake handle and jumped down. He strode to the open door of the rambling log ranch house.

"Anybody home?" he called.

There was no answer. He called again. Finally he heard feet shuffling in another room. A Chinese appeared in a door that evidently led to the kitchen. He stood there for a while, cleaning his dough-sticky hands on his long white apron.

"'Lo, what you want, hey?" he asked, running the short words together so they sounded like one long one.

"I'm looking for the boss, Rex Benton."

"Boss man? Miz Benton maybe down by bunkhouse I don' know."

A voice from another room: "Here I am, Ah Toy."

From the way Rex Benton spoke a person could tell he was used to being obeyed. His was a strong voice, a voice of authority. Following it, his step was confident and loud. They expected a large man, but he wasn't: he was short, broad, and vigorous. He looked them over for a second with eyes that seemed a little sharp, and a little cold.

He asked: "Are you looking for me?"

"If you're Rex Benton, we are. I'm Dusty Sears, your new foreman, and this is Yakima, my top hand."

Benton seemed to flinch, but he instantly recovered his composure. His lips parted in a broad smile — a cordial smile — a smile of welcome. But his eyes were still as hard as knife steel. "Glad you got here. I didn't know you were coming so soon or I'd have sent the buckboard in for you." He advanced and extended his hand.

"Didn't you get his letter?" Dusty asked.

"Who? T. H. Hawley's? Did he write? Well now, if he did, I didn't get it. The boys were down to the mailbox only a couple of days ago, too. Our box is down by the stage road, and sometimes the driver forgets. Stage drivers are that way. Well, no use crying about spilt milk. How's T.H.?"

They talked about the Old Man for a while, and about affairs at the capital. Benton then showed them the foreman's house. It was a two-room place, built of cottonwood logs. Next to it was the bunkhouse. None of the boys seemed to be around.

"I'd like to meet up with the boys," said Dusty. "Will they be in for supper?"

"Not tonight."

"Tomorrow?"

"No. You'll have to wait around a few days."

"Where are they?"

"They're out on a roundup."

Roundup! Dusty knew that the Wagonhammer association had finished its roundup a month before. He maintained a pokerface, but Benton must have sensed his suspicion.

He explained: "Little private roundup of our own. The rustlers have been up to their usual tricks lately. Tucker gang. And those murders, too. You heard about them? They're the work of the Tucker gang if you want my opinion. They hung Oren Tucker back in the Windy Ridge two or three years back, but I said then we weren't finished with them."

"What range is the roundup working?"

Benton was evasive.

Dusty asked: "Got a couple of horses to spare? I'll lope on over tonight and get acquainted."

Benton set his lips in a thin, hard line. "No, better stay here for a while."

"Reckon the foreman's place is with the men."

Benton whirled and faced him. His cloak of cordiality slipped from him. His thumb significantly hung in his belt just over the polished walnut stocks of his six-shooter. "I'm sorry, Sears," he said in a voice that was drained of color. "You're foreman here. But I'm still manager. Understand that? I'm manager. And I say you don't go."

It was a tight moment. Nobody breathed for the space of two or three seconds. Then Dusty's easy drawl broke the tension. "That's right, Benton," he said with a smile, "you're manager and I'm foreman. Those are the big boss's words. So, if you say I don't go tonight, then I don't go."

Yakima, listening tensely, didn't miss his partner's use of the word *tonight*.

Benton nodded. "Just so we understand each other," he said crisply. He turned on his toe and strode to the house without a backward glance.

"*Hmm*," said Yakima musingly, smoothing down his six red hairs, "I'd guess that one at twelve rattles and a button."

They fed the cayuse team and wandered around the corrals. While doing this, they caught sight of a rider who approached from the direction of Dry River. He didn't come near the corrals — he rode to the rear of the ranch house, then, in less than a minute, he rode away again. Light from the setting sun reflected silvery from one of his holsters just before he disappeared.

"Somethin' familiar about him," Yakima said, twisting his face thoughtfully.

Dusty agreed. "Funny how often that silvery gun shine has been showin' up since we first run into that Basette varmint. Very funny about lots of things. For instance . . . why were we put off that coach and told to vamoose? And what would Cibber want with two wagonloads of dynamite? Why did he want to pay our way out of the country? How did he know I was the new foreman of the Circle Two and three hundred a month was exactly twice what the Old Man was paying me? Funny we were shot at . . .."

"And lucky we was missed," murmured Yakima.

"And now Benton, here . . . how did he know I was to be his new foreman if he didn't get the Old Man's letter? And why does he want to keep us here at the ranch? There's something funny going on around here, all right."

"Very funny, indeed," said Yakima.

"There's a few things I'd like to find out about that north range where those killings have been. I'd like to see that glacial dam that keeps water flowing down the Wagonhammer and not down Furnace Creek. Maybe we ought to take a ride up that way. Sort of quiet . . . start tomorrow, couple of hours before sunup . . . while our good friend Rex Benton is deep in slumber."

They were miles from the ranch when the sun's edge showed over the low peaks of the Windy Ridge Mountains. Yakima, who had been preoccupied for the last mile or two, finally broke his silence.

"You notice that fancy saddle which was hangin' over the corral gate last night?"

"Sure. It was a nice chocolate brown . . . a Meeney I'd guess. Had a set of longhorns tooled on the cantle."

"That was no company saddle."

All the Old Man's saddles were made by an outfit in Denver. They were light-tanned, low-shelled with the brand **O-2** burned just behind the horn. As all cowboys had their own, the Old Man had furnished just a few for emergencies.

"No, that wasn't a company saddle," Dusty agreed.

"And it wasn't the Chinaboy's saddle."

"You're tryin' to say that it was Benton's saddle."

"Exactly. And when we left this mornin', it wasn't there."

Dusty's eyes became hard and thoughtful. Benton must have left ahead of them. He wondered what for.

Their trail followed the Wagonhammer for another mile or two. Then it turned to join a wagon road that forded the stream and climbed steeply up to the bench land. The road had been well traveled in recent days. Up ahead they caught sight of a ten-mule team pulling two wagons in tandem. The outfit was just completing the last leg of its climb from the creek level. It seemed familiar, and its driver did, too. In a minute they caught up with it. They recognized Milk River Jordan.

Dusty hailed him. "Hello, Milk River."

"Whoa!" Milk River laid back on his two fistfuls of lines. "Whoa, you Missouri mavericks." He turned and squinted at them. "Well, if it ain't the walkin' cowboys! You've traveled a smart piece since I left you off in Dry River t'other night." He rubbed his stubble and looked at them.

Dusty sized up the load. "See you're out early with your blackjack eatin' tobacco."

Milk River gazed thoughtfully back at the canvas-shrouded wagons. "Yep, up with the owls. Makin' an early delivery for Ezra Cibber, the Dry River philanthropist. Four hundred and forty-four cases of blackstrap eatin' tobacco for the Tucker gang. C.O.D. delivery. Gettin' paid off in Wells Fargo gold and Circle Two mavericks . . . them latter to stock the Furnace Flat range, driest patch of alkali this side of Hades."

Milk River spoke lightly, but his sun-squinty eyes were hard. While he talked, he wrapped his reins around the tall hand brake, and now he sat with his palms resting significantly near his gun butts. But he had no cause to fear — Dusty and Yakima had a certain affection for their former benefactor and had no intention of causing him trouble.

Dusty asked: "Where do you go to hunt the Tuckers?"

"Ain't you heard about them Tuckers? You don't need to go huntin' them. If you got somethin' the Tucker boys want, they hunt you. Now, f'instance, the Tuckers are right anxious to get this here eatin' tobacco. 'Specially old Gramp Tucker . . . he's strong for eatin' tobacco. Eats it straight, fried, or stewed like jerky. So, wantin' it, the boys keep a close eye peeled when they're expectin' a shipment. Can't tell a speck about it. One of them Tuckers may have you in the V of his gun sights right now from a-hind that rock." Milk River spat significantly in the direction of a large granite boulder a few rods away. "Or, he might be a-hind that prairie dog hill. And a Tucker is plenty itchy in the trigger finger when he sees his eatin' tobacco bein' trailed too close." Milk River unfastened his lines. "Well, it's been good seein' you, but I got to mosey. Git up you long-eared sons-o'-Satan afore I sell you to the

Injuns!" The long lash sang through the air and cracked like a .30-30. The mules humped forward. The wagon wheels creaked.

Yakima and Dusty sat their horses and watched the outfit roll slowly away across the bench land.

Yakima asked: "Did he mean there really *was* Tuckers?"

"Not likely. I don't think there's a Tucker gang at all. Milk River has a load of dynamite, and I don't need more'n one guess as to what it's intended for." They started on. "But, Tuckers or no Tuckers, I don't imagine it would be healthy to trail him too close."

They left the wagon road and followed a shallow, greasewood-filled draw that wound in the direction of the mountains. The sun climbed higher, rebounded hotly from the rocky, whitish soil. They were headed into a plainless country of sharp-sided gulches and wind-carved pinnacles of rock.

Suddenly Dusty reined in. "Listen!" he said.

They could hear the distant popping of gunfire. Then silence. They turned down a dry wash that seemed to lead in the direction of the sound. There was one more shot — louder. Suddenly the dry wash fanned out on a wide bench. They pulled in. Down below were four riders; two of them dismounted and examined some object on the ground. In a few minutes they rode away. The object was still there.

"That's a man," said Dusty. "A dead man."

"Another dead man on the north range!"

When the four riders disappeared, they rode to where he lay. They dismounted, examined him. He was an old man, long-whiskered, white-haired. He was dressed in rough miner's clothes. A battered hat lay a few yards away. The front of his faded gray shirt was crusted blackly with blood.

"That man wasn't shot today," said Dusty. "He's probably been here since yesterday."

"He must have been killed today."

"Why?"

"Didn't we hear shootin'?"

"Sure. That's what makes it so strange. One more funny thing to chalk up. Here's a lot of shootin' and a day-old dead man. Say, maybe . . ."

"Maybe what?"

"I have an idea that shootin' was mainly for our benefit."

Like an exclamation point to his words, a bullet smacked the ground close to him and whined away. There was no cover. They were baffled for a moment, not knowing where to turn. Yakima started to mount, but Dusty stopped him.

"Lie flat!"

They flopped prone on the ground. Here they were momentarily safe, hidden by a nearby swell in the ground. A couple of bullets droned just above them. They glanced around. The only possible protection was a jumbled heap of rock thirty paces away.

Dusty pointed toward it. "Crawl as far as you can. Then run like the Blackfeet were after you."

They snaked slowly along the ground, bodies flat. The sage tore at their faces and at their clothes. Alkali dust gritted in their teeth. They crawled beyond the protecting bulge of ground, but the sage still hid them. They chanced crawling a few more yards. The heap of rocks was now only ten or twelve paces distant.

A bullet plowed the earth in front of them, sending out a stinging shower of dirt and rock pellets. They sprinted for the rocks, flung themselves in their shelter. A rattlesnake sounded off right at Yakima's elbow. He almost jumped into the open again.

"Blast 'em, they're all after us today," he panted.

Dusty grinned. "Yakima, you leave that snake alone." He looked at the snake with a musing expression. "You know, I used to think rattlers was an ornery lot, but, durin' these last two days I've got wind of so many varmints which was worse I'd as soon take that belly-crawlin' critter to church with me." He rolled a cigarette and looked at the coiled snake with tolerance. "Yes, sir, you can say one thing for a rattler . . . the head end of him is old pizen for sure, but the tail end of him is right decent."

The firing was sporadic. Now and then a bullet struck one of the rocks, glanced, whined away into space. They fired back at the puffs of smoke that rose and hung in the still air close to some sandstone pillars near the edge of the flat.

Dusty's .41-caliber gun carried up well, but firing at gunsmoke was like firing at flashes in the dark — maybe worse. He stopped after a third of his belt had been consumed. He sat there, thinking.

"Funny," he said.

"What's funny now?"

"Funny they ain't shot our horses. Seems like that would be the first thing they'd do if they didn't want us to get away. And something else, Yakima, them buckos are shootin' Thirty-Thirties. A person can bead down pretty close from the range with a Winchester, and none of their slugs has more'n come close. Appears like they didn't want to hit us at all."

"I wouldn't want to take a stroll to find out," Yakima grumbled.

The firing stopped. A few minutes later they caught sight of the four riders loping away along the crest of a hogback. It appeared safe, so they caught their horses.

"Back to the ranch?" asked Yakima.

"I doubt it would be healthy. I think it would be a good idea to go down and chin with Leona's paw. Can't tell, Jim Brant might have a line on these doings. Anyway, he'll be honest, I'll lay gold to greenbacks on that."

CHAPTER
FIVE

It was a long trip ahead, so they rode slowly to save their horses. They didn't talk much. The only sound was the regular *hiss* of the sage, greasewood, and buffalo grass under the hoofs, the dull *creak* of saddle leather, and the *click-click* of spur chains against the stirrups. Toward evening, after miles of silence, Yakima burst out.

"Corn fritters! Yum-yum! Have I ever told you how my maw could make corn fritters? How I'd like a plate of 'em now, swimmin' in sorghum!"

"You hungry? Why, Yakima, you ate only yesterday."

"Hungry! My backbone's sawin' against my stomach like a Cree fiddle."

A light glimmered in the twilight that was settling on the valley of the Wagonhammer. This must be Brant's. They rode up to a side window, looked in. The room they saw was large, lace-curtained, well-furnished. Most ranchers lit their homes with common bacon-grease dips, but the Brants boasted an ornate kerosene lamp, one with a reflector that hung in a wall bracket. A woman sat near a table, sewing; it was Leona. Nearer to the lamp a gray-haired man was leafing through a booklet.

They dismounted and rapped. Leona came to the door. She stood there for a second before recognizing them. Her hair was coppery with the light of the lamp shining through it.

"Why, it's Dusty and Yakima," she said, smiling. The gray-haired man laid down his booklet and came toward them. "Dad, these are the new men from the Circle Two . . . you know, the ones I rode from town with."

Jim Brant greeted them cordially. Later on, after they did justice to an excellent supper that Leona prepared, Dusty and Brant went to the room that was used as a ranch office, and seated themselves for a talk. Brant had closed the door, but a moment later it swung open and a young man walked in.

Brant said: "This is Rollie, my stepson. Rollie, meet Dusty Sears, new foreman at the Circle Two. He was sent up by my old friend, T. H. Hawley." Then to Dusty: "You can go ahead and talk in front of Rollie. I'll guarantee him."

Dusty was uncomfortable despite the assurance. He wanted to talk to Jim Brant alone. He noticed Rollie's eyes rest again and again on the .41-caliber gun. What could be so interesting about it? Each time Dusty glanced up, Rollie would look quickly away. Still, if Brant guaranteed him . . .

Dusty gave a brief account of everything that had happened since his arrival — but only the surface, the actual events, no opinions.

Brant smiled when mention was made of Ezra Cibber and his plan to run cattle on the Furnace Flat range. "Don't take Cibber too seriously. He's queer, but he's harmless. I know he has ideas about ranching down there. He used to stick to that store like a badger to his hole . . . hardly go anywhere . . . but lately he's taken to riding all over the country. Well, if he thinks he can make money grazing that dry-bone range, that's his funeral. And as for those killings up on the north range, they're the work of the Tucker gang, in my opinion. Those Tuckers were never all cleaned out. I always said they'd be back and it looks like I'm right."

Here was Brant talking about the Tucker gang. After his meeting that morning with Milk River Jordan, Dusty had decided no such gang existed. And if it did, why would a gang of rustlers murder a rancher like Cyrus Woolridge and not run off his cattle? And there was the poor old fellow they ran onto that afternoon — he wasn't a cattleman at all; he was a prospector, unless Dusty missed his guess. Why would anyone kill him? And he recalled the words of the lanky cowboy who was on the coach from Split Rock — "If you want my idea, old Cy found out something he shouldn't."

It all fit together quite well with the suspicion that lurked deeply in Dusty's mind — a suspicion he had not yet voiced. He had ridden down to take up that suspicion with Brant. He hated to mention it while Rollie was in the room. Still, Brant said Rollie could be trusted.

Dusty started out: "We caught a ride on a peculiar sort of freight load going to Dry River the other night."

Brant waited expectantly. Rollie's eyes shifted around more than ever.

Dusty went on: "Very strange. I guessed it to be two wagonloads of dynamite."

"Wagonloads? Who would want two wagonloads of dynamite in Dry River?"

"Ezra Cibber."

Brant considered. "Well, he runs a store. I suppose he'd sell it. It still seems like a large order, but, as I said, the old fellow's getting queer of late."

"He isn't selling it. Just from curiosity, I went down there next day and tried to buy a few sticks. Said he never handled it."

Brant waited for Dusty to go on. Rollie nervously twisted his fine, light sombrero.

"The dynamite wasn't unloaded in Dry River at all. We ran onto it again this morning. It was headed for the north range."

"What possible use would there be for it there?"

"We were aiming on finding that out ourselves, but some boys with Winchesters made it a bit interesting for a spell."

Brant's pipe had gone out, but he puffed without noticing. His voice was tight when he asked: "What do you think the dynamite was intended for?"

"What do *I* think? I think Ezra Cibber and some other fellows are planning to turn the Furnace Flat into something besides a dry-bone range."

Nobody spoke for a few seconds. The only sound was the squeak of Rollie's chair as he moved his weight uncomfortably from one side to the other.

Then Brant asked in a low, tense voice: "You mean they intend to blast out that glacial dam . . . the one that keeps the water flowing down the Wagonhammer?"

"It's a thought," Dusty said.

Jim Brant jumped to his feet, clomped back and forth across the room a few times, then he sat heavily in his chair.

"They couldn't do it! They couldn't do it without somebody finding out."

"Maybe Woolridge found out. Or that fellow who was shot before him. And that old prospector we found today . . . maybe they all found out. I can't see any other reason for anyone killing them."

"They wouldn't dare! We'd hang 'em to the highest cottonwood on the Wagonhammer."

Dusty thoughtfully rolled a cigarette. "You'd hang 'em," he said calmly, "*provided* you had more men than they did. But if more men stand to benefit by having water in Furnace Creek than in the Wagonhammer . . . what then?"

Jim Brant didn't answer. He sat there, staring at Dusty, sucking at his extinct pipe.

They had both forgotten about Rollie. They were reminded of him when he stood up. He fumbled with his crumpled hat. Then he edged toward the door. He mumbled something, quickly stepped out, closed the door after him.

Conversation lagged. Dusty had given the elder man something considerable to think about. A breeze puffed out the window's white starched curtain. How quiet it was! From outside Dusty could hear the shrill chirp of a cricket, the distant wail of a coyote, and the quiet murmur of the Wagonhammer. Then, from somewhere, his ear picked up a dull, scraping sound, such as gates make when dragged open across hoof-powdered corral dirt. Then the click of spur or bit chains. He listened, suddenly alert. The seconds dragged on to minutes. The curtain shook in the breeze. Brant stared at the floor, puffing his pipe. Again the coyote howled. Dusty relaxed. It was nothing, he decided.

Then, distantly but unmistakably, he heard the noise of galloping hoofs. They slowly faded away. Galloping in the dark! Whoever it was must be in a hurry. Nothing short of a stampede could make most cowboys gallop their horses on a night as dark as this.

Dusty and Yakima were shown upstairs to the Brants' guest room. Its furnishings were homemade but comfortable. There was an easy chair made chiefly of woven willow branches, a hat rack constructed of polished buffalo horns — a Cree squaw's masterpiece — and, against the wall, a bed. The bed consisted of a frame over which a steer's hide had been laced — rawhide that, in drying, became stretched as tightly as a drum head. On it was a tick filled with fresh rushes. A man floating on a cloud could have been no more comfortable than on this bed — Dusty and Yakima went to sleep almost instantly.

Dusty had no idea how long he slept. But suddenly he was awake, staring into the darkness. What had awakened him? He listened tensely. Yakima, lying beside him, breathed regularly.

Then his ear picked up low sounds out in the ranch yard. The *clip-clop* of shod hoofs, the low creak of leather, the cricket in somebody's bit. He got up quickly and looked from the window. A large cottonwood whose branches overhung the window and the roof of the house hid most of the yard from view, but through a few ragged openings among the leaves he made out several shadow shapes moving in the faded moonlight. There were no voices.

He recalled Rollie's sudden departure. A trap!

He shook Yakima.

"What the . . . ?" Yakima started in a voice that seemed to boom in the taut silence. Dusty quieted him.

"There's something brewing up outside, and I think it's some poison intended for us."

They quickly slipped into their clothes, glanced again outside. The riders were at the house now. Yakima started for the door. Dusty stopped him.

"They'll have the house surrounded."

Someone rode beneath the tree, stopping right beneath the window. The moonlight reflected dully from his bridle trappings. He dismounted, strode to the door, beat against the casing with his fist.

"Brant! Jim Brant!" It was a strange voice.

Brant's voice came from inside the house: "Who is it?"

"Bob Till."

The name was familiar. Where had he heard of a man named Till? Then he remembered — the story of the Woolridge murder in the *Spit Rock Review*: "Sheriff

Till has taken a posse to the Wagonhammer country . . ."

There was an interval of silence while Brant was coming to the door. He said: "Hello, Sheriff. Isn't this a little bit late for the law?"

"It's never too late to run down dry-gulchers."

"You won't find any here."

"I'm not so sure. Didn't a couple of strange 'punchers visit you here tonight?"

"Only the new foreman from the Circle Two and his top hand."

"They're likely the ones. A tall fellow named Dusty and a short one with a shiny dome . . . ?"

"*They're* not dry-gulchers!"

"No?" The sheriff's tone indicated he had proof. "Jim, there was an old prospector shot and killed on the north range this afternoon. And we know it was a Forty-One-caliber gun that killed him. He was ambushed from behind a nest of rocks . . . a dirty, sneaking job if I ever saw one. We found plenty of empty Forty-One cartridges laying around. And I happen to know that tall fellow who visited you carried that caliber gun."

"Anybody can carry a Forty-One."

"That's true. They ain't common, but there's no law ag'in' 'em. However, four riders from the Circle Two came up and saw 'em when they was leavin' the scene, so there's no mistake about who did it."

They could hear the door open and close when the sheriff went inside.

Dusty leaned from the window. The foliage of the cottonwood hung around him like a dark veil. One of the tree's large limbs was within reach. He took it, swung out. The limb swayed gently with his weight, but the only sound was a slight rustle of leaves. He crawled along until he reached the trunk, waited. The limb swayed again. Dusty could feel it jiggle, so he knew that Yakima was coming, although it was too dark to see until their bodies almost touched. They didn't dare speak — not four feet below them was a man on horseback. Dusty could have touched the man's hat with his toe. The horse shifted positions and the rider muttered some indistinguishable word. Another man rode up, dismounted, went inside. He spoke. They recognized the voice — Benton's.

Dusty pointed to Benton's horse, tied near the door. Then he pointed to the rider who sat just beneath them. He could tell by a responding tenseness of Yakima's body that he got the idea.

Dusty pulled his six-shooter from the holster. He held it flat in the palm of his hand, swung down, clinging to the limb by the other hand and his legs. The man was close, so close Dusty could smell the perspiration that stuck to his shirt.

Not too hard, Dusty told himself, *and not too easy . . . but just right.*

He swung the six-gun. It struck solidly. The man made no sound when the cold metal struck him. There was just a reflex tightening of muscles, then he sagged. He would have slipped from his horse if Dusty hadn't grabbed him. It all happened so silently that another rider, sitting his horse only eight or nine yards away didn't notice.

Dusty held the rider to his horse. Yakima dropped to the ground, ran quickly over, untied Benton's horse, mounted. Then Dusty flung aside the sagging rider. The horse reared, but his new master was in the saddle. A quick twist at the bridle and the horse came down, running.

"Hey, Red, what's the trouble?" somebody shouted.

The only answer was the sound of hoofs racing across the ranch yard and away along the trail.

Dusty and Yakima followed the trail for only a few hundred yards, then they plunged into a brushy gully. Five minutes later they felt safe to stop. They reined in and looked around at the lonely, moon-swept prairie.

"Well, Yakima," said Dusty, "you are now a fugitive from the law."

CHAPTER
SIX

When the posse left in pursuit of Dusty and Yakima, Jim Brant went back to bed and tried to sleep. After tossing for an hour, he got up and brewed coffee. Leona found him still sitting there in the morning, a half-filled cup of coffee, now gone stone cold, on the table in front of him.

She asked: "You don't think Dusty shot that prospector, do you?"

He shook his head. "Of course not. Both those boys are on the level. But there's something going on around here that makes more sense than it looks like on the surface."

"I can't see what sense there can be in murdering men like Cyrus Woolridge and that old prospector."

"Maybe it's like Dusty said . . . maybe they found out something they shouldn't." He took a swallow of cold coffee. "There are a couple other things that don't have much sense to them, too. But they fit together pretty well . . . for instance, two wagonloads of dynamite and the Furnace Flat range." He stood up with the air of one who has come to a decision. "I'm going to send Rollie out to call in the Wagonhammer ranchers for a meeting . . . here . . . tonight."

★ ★ ★

That night there were many men gathered at the Brant Ranch. Cowpunchers, men from the posse, and Benton's men congregated on the bench in front of the bunkhouse and along the poles of the corrals.

After supper, the ranchers of the Wagonhammer range met in Jim Brant's office. There was Brant, sitting at the desk, Rex Benton at his right; other chairs were occupied by Joel Sims, Williams of the Bar Diamond, and Buckland of the C-B. They waited tensely for the news Jim Brant had for them. They knew it was no idle fancy that prompted him to send for them.

Brant looked around. "Well, we're all here. I suppose you're wondering what all this is about. Most of you probably think it's about those killings we've been having lately. In a way it is. But it isn't so much the killings as it is the *reason* behind the killings."

The five men waited expectantly. Rex Benton was inscrutable. When Brant paused, Benton glanced nervously at the darkness outside the window. Noting his glance, Brant looked at the window, too. Benton then steadfastly kept his eyes on the floor in front of his feet.

Brant went on: "I wonder if any of you ever considered the possibility of the Wagonhammer drying up? Not just for a month or two, but for good. Maybe you're like me . . . you never considered it because you never thought it possible. But it is possible."

Rex Benton drew from his pocket a white handkerchief, shook it in front of him several times, then used it to wipe away the perspiration from under his shirt collar.

Brant was saying: "I happened to run onto some facts the other night, at least I believe they're facts . . ."

Something clinked through the window, whipped the air of the room, struck home with a little *thud*. Outside there was the report of a gun. Brant's sentence broke off. He stood, spun on his toes, clutched for a second at the back of a chair. Then the life went out of him, and he sprawled limply across the rough board floor.

He was dead before any in the room — save perhaps one — realized what had happened. Shocked speechless, they stared at him. In the distance a horse galloped.

Men were shouting outside. The ranchers rushed from the room. Down by the corral, several cowpunchers were tossing saddles on horses. They would pursue, although the darkness made it useless.

Rex Benton did not come out at first. He was there a half a minute later. He strode with purpose, his face hard and determined, and he carried some object in his hand.

He announced: "Men, here's the bullet that killed Jim Brant. It's a Forty-One caliber. You don't happen to know anyone who carries a Forty-One caliber, do you?"

His words were followed by a tense silence. One of the ranchers spoke up.

"You bet we know a fellow who carries a Forty-One. And we'll run the varmint to ground before the sun sets tomorrow or you can call me an Injun. It's past time a few cottonwoods was sproutin' fruit hereabouts. Nobody can murder a man like Jim Brant and get away with it."

"You say my father has been murdered?"

It was Leona's voice. She was facing them there, a few steps in front of the door, erect, poker-faced. For a few seconds nobody answered. Then Joel Sims fumblingly took off his hat and made a step forward.

"Yes, Miss Leona. Your paw has been shot down."

"Who did it?" she asked in a colorless voice.

"That tall stranger we put off the coach a couple days ago."

"Did you see him?"

"No, ma'am. We didn't exactly see him. But we got proof he's a killer, and your paw was shot down by a Forty-One-caliber gun. The tall stranger is the only one hereabouts who carries that brand of weapon."

"That's no proof!" In excitement, her voice raised a little. She seemed to be on the point of breaking down. "Anybody could have shot a Forty-One just to lay the blame on him. Nobody *saw* him."

A man came forward out of the darkness. The light from the door reflected from his two silver-mounted guns. It was Basette. He was doing his best to assume a straightforward honest appearance, but his eyes were still thin and shifty.

He said: "*I* saw him. I caught sight of him from behind the barn just when he started to ride away." It was evident that she doubted him, so he quickly went on: "But I'm not the only one. You don't need to believe me. Your own stepbrother saw him, too."

Benton asked: "Where is he?"

"Down by the barn."

"Bring him up!"

It was a minute before Rollie got there. He looked sick, like a man suffering from ptomaine poisoning. His face had gone fish-belly white and large beads of perspiration stood on his upper lip. His legs wobbled and he might not have been able to stand at all had not Basette been helping him. He stood there for a few seconds, the light from the ranch house door showing how pale he was. He couldn't meet Leona's eyes. He glanced toward the window of Jim Brant's office — the window with the little round hole through it — and then looked quickly away.

"Guess he feels pretty bad," Benton said. Then with a voice that contained a note of command: "Rollie! Buck up!" He stepped over and shook Rollie by the shoulder. "Hear me? Buck up! Tell us what you saw."

He turned on Benton with a sudden show of will; their eyes met. Rollie had started to say something, but it was evident he changed his mind. He quailed before Benton's glance.

Benton spoke again: "Did you see that tall fellow, Dusty Sears?"

Rollie nodded.

"And the short fellow with the peeled scalp . . . Yakima?"

"Yes," Rollie managed to say, "I saw them both."

Benton nodded to Basette. "All right." He spoke with exaggerated sympathy. "Poor kid, he's hard hit. Take him inside and fix him something to drink."

When Rollie turned to go, his eyes met Leona's. She could tell by their pleading expression that he wanted to say more.

59

★ ★ ★

An hour passed. Leona sat by the parlor table, trying to adjust herself to the brutal fact of her father's death, trying also to comprehend all the things that had happened during the last few days. Somehow, even after Rollie said what he did about Dusty, she couldn't think of that tall, easy-talking cowboy as a murderer — as the murderer of her father. She had an unusual feeling toward Dusty from the first time they met, from the moment her eyes spotted him stepping down from the coach that rainy afternoon at Bedrock station.

Still pondering, she took a lamp and climbed the stairs to her room. She noticed something lying on her pillow. It was a scrap of paper, folded. She hurried to open it. Some words were scribbled in pencil. She recognized the hand as Rollie's.

I'll be waiting for you at Bald Rock. Midnight. Very important.

Rollie

She glanced at her lapel watch. It was quarter past eleven. Then she still had time — Bald Rock was about three miles distant. She hurriedly changed to boots and riding skirt, ran downstairs. She didn't take a light, but found her way by habit through the darkened rooms and out the back door. She met no one on her way to the corrals. A bacon-grease dip burned in the bunkhouse where the cowboys were playing stud poker. She could hear the jingle of coins when she walked past, avoiding the streak of yellow light that fell from the door. She entered the barn. It was dark as the depths of a mine — so dark it seemed to flicker before her eyes. She felt her way. Her saddle was not where she expected it to be. Suddenly she was positive there was someone standing near her. She restrained a mad impulse to run, turned, and at that instant someone struck a match.

"Who's there?" It was Benton's voice. She recognized his hard face in the spluttering flame of the sulphur match. "You, Miss Leona. What are you doing here?"

She stammered. She didn't want to tell about Rollie's note. She didn't want anyone to know about their meeting. "I'm going for a ride," she finally said.

He shot a sharp glance at her. "Not tonight!"

She got control of herself. Why should this man interfere? "Yes! Certainly I can go for a ride if I choose!"

"I'm sorry," he said. "I didn't mean to interfere. Naturally this is your ranch and you're your own boss. I was only surprised."

"I need some air."

"Sure," he said. In the last glimmer of the match she saw that his eyes were suspicious. "I'll get one of the boys to help you saddle up."

He called one of the men from the bunkhouse. He watched while the man led her rangy gelding from a stall and saddled it. Benton made her uneasy. It was too dark to see, but when she mounted and rode away, it seemed as if his eyes, like a cat's, were following her.

Once away from the building, a blue, faded starlight lit the prairie's main features. In the distance, against the night sky, she could make out the ragged silhouette of Bald Rock. She still had plenty of time before midnight so she didn't hurry. Her horse climbed the steep slope that led to the rock. The moonlight shone briefly on it from a rift in the clouds. The rock was forty or fifty feet high, dome-shaped in general outline, but with large weather cracks that cut deeply into it like miniature cañons. These were in black shadow, contrasting with the outer surfaces that seemed white like snow in the half light.

She listened. A sound had caused her horse to lift his head and stare back in the direction from which they had come. She couldn't tell what it was, the clatter of a loose stone, perhaps. She decided it must be Rollie.

"Rollie!" she called.

There was no answer. She listened for the sound of a horse. Her own mount was no longer interested — he reached down and cropped off a mouthful of buffalo grass and stood chewing it against his bit.

"Rollie!" she called, louder than before.

She waited. Minutes dragged. Her watch said quarter past twelve. She rode around the rocks. He did not come at 12:30, or at 12:45. It was after 1:00 when she started back, sick with uncertainty.

All morning, following their escape from Sheriff Till and his posse, Dusty and Yakima rode north along the Wagonhammer.

Dusty remarked: "I aim to see that glacial dam with my own eyes. Then, if they're fixin' to blast it out, as I expect they are, we'd better ride like Injuns to Split

Rock. There's a telegraph line there. We'll send a message to the Old Man. We can't do much . . . just the two of us against the whole country."

"What can the Old Man do?"

Dusty chuckled. "What'll he do? I wouldn't be surprised if he climbed right out of that wheelchair, rheumatics or no. Either that or get the governor to round up his cavalry."

Yakima was riding Benton's horse, a fine, large-barreled bay, and a steady traveler. Dusty had a small cayuse, willing and prairie-wise as are all his breed, but his owner had shod him with rawhide — improvised boots drawn around the hoofs and dried tightly — a poor job that had caused the animal to go footsore.

They were forced to travel slowly, and in consequence it was late afternoon when they approached the place where the glacial dam had turned the water from Furnace Flat into the Wagonhammer. This was dangerous ground — the north range where killers had already cut down three men. Avoiding the high ground, they followed a succession of dry washes that roughly paralleled the main stream. The country was briefly visible when they rode from the head end of one dry wash and headed into another. Dusty pointed toward a white line that snaked up from the Wagonhammer. It was the road. But what caught his interest was not the road; it was a string of dark dots, and, following them, two large rectangles. They crept slowly.

He said: "If that ain't Milk River Jordan's outfit, you can call me a sheepherder. Looks like he's headed for town."

Dusty estimated they were now a trifle above the position of the glacial dam. They followed a saddle in the bench to another dry wash, then they turned and dropped down toward the Wagonhammer. They were close now. Neither spoke. They rode cautiously.

Dusty's cayuse, shod as it was with rawhide, made scarcely a sound, but the steel shoes on Yakima's mount clattered dangerously loud on the rocks that paved the bottom of the draw. He tried to keep in the soft dirt up the banks.

They were getting close now. Every moment they half expected some sniper's gun to crack from behind a rock or a clump of greasewood. The dry wash became deeper. Its walls towered steeply over them. They were nearing the Wagonhammer.

Dusty reined in: "Listen!"

They could hear a regular creaking, chugging sound. It seemed to come from around the next turn in the dry wash. It was the kind of a sound a well-drilling rig makes in raising and dropping its bit into the soil.

Dusty dismounted, handed his reins to Yakima. He paused to drop a cartridge into the empty chamber beneath the hammer of his gun. Then he went on.

Yakima, left alone, nervously lifted his hat and, with the same hand, smoothed down his six red hairs. Perspiration made them stick to his scalp.

Dusty expected to find the source of the sound when he made the turn in the dry wash, but it was still farther on. It was louder — a creak followed by a thump, over and over.

He moved more cautiously. The wash made a sharp turn to the right. He started around, then flattened himself against the wall. A man was standing there, not thirty feet distant.

Dusty stood for a second or two in plain sight, but the man did not look up. He was intently splicing a piece of rope. Dusty edged from view, retraced a dozen steps, then he climbed the steep side of the wash. The guarded branches of a greasewood offered protection. He lay prone and surveyed the scene below.

As he guessed, it was a well-drilling rig. Two horses, hitched to a whim, walked in a beaten circle. The bit rose and fell regularly. He could make out the outline of the glacial dam stretching across the ancient, wide valley of Furnace Creek, turning the water into the newer, sharper valley of the Wagonhammer. On the crest of the dam stood the well-drilling rig. Many circular paths, hoof-worn, showed where other holes had been sunk. Dusty could see how these holes, loaded with dynamite and exploded in unison, would tear asunder the glacial dam simultaneously opening Furnace Creek and filling the Wagonhammer with dirt and rubble. But there was still time to stop them. Judging by the dynamite stacked in cases on the dam, they were by no means through drilling.

He slid back down the dry wash and hurried to where Yakima waited.

"They're fixing to blast it, just like we supposed," he said grimly. "You light out and ride like blazes. You'll have to go without me. My horse is too footsore. Rustle yourself another mount at the Circle Two. If you ride

65

hard, maybe you can be in Split Rock to send that telegram to the Old Man by tomorrow morning. Send it, and then come back. I'll meet you by that dome-shaped rock of Brant's in two days."

Yakima spurred away in the direction of the Circle 2 at the fastest pace the chestnut could endure. It was night when he got there. The only light was in the kitchen. The Chinese cook sat at a table playing solitaire. The bunkhouse was empty. He roped a fresh horse, saddled, hurried on. He followed the trail that skirted the brushy Wagonhammer for several miles, then he swung to higher ground in order to avoid Brant's ranch.

This course took him close to the bald rock. That was where he would meet Dusty two days hence. A movement off in the dark caused him to rein in. He listened. Voices! One was high-pitched, almost like a boy's. It was familiar. He tried to place it. And the other voice — he knew that. It was Basette's. The high-pitched voice quavered with pleading, but only now and then was a word distinguishable.

Two shots knifed the darkness. That was all — two shots. After a while, galloping hoofs. Then silence.

Yakima sat there a minute or two. Then he slowly rode toward the place where the gun had flashed.

"Hey, over there!" he called.

There was no answer. He dismounted and walked slowly around the rock. The moon floated through a rift in the clouds. There, scarcely a rod away, was a man, face down, one hand clutching buffalo grass.

Yakima rolled him over. He started with surprise. It was Rollie — Jim Brant's adopted son. Dead — shot twice, forehead and chest.

Somewhere in the vast, prairie darkness a hoof clattered on a rock. Yakima quickly mounted and rode away.

Dusty's orders had been to ride hell-bent for the Split Rock telegraph office, but Dusty hadn't considered anything like the murder of Rollie Brant taking place. So Yakima headed for the Brant Ranch. He stopped when it came in view. Lights burned in an upstairs window and the bunkhouse. The yard down there seemed full of shadow movement. Something unusual must be going on tonight.

A light bobbing with walking rhythm along the ground — that was someone carrying a lantern. The light stopped bobbing and hung still, illuminating a few poles of the corral. From time to time men's shadows would pass, momentarily cutting off its wind-flickery light. In fifteen or twenty minutes the light went out. Soon the moon sailed from the curdled night clouds to disclose a file of men on horseback moving up the valley trail toward the Circle 2. Then all was quiet. He could risk riding down there now.

His horse slid down a steep bank tangled with rose briars, splashed through the shallow stream, then up and across the wide, deserted yard. He dismounted under the cottonwood tree and tiptoed inside. The front room was dark save for the shaft of light that came from the slightly open door to Brant's office. He went to the door, peeped in. Shocked, he drew back. Brant lay there, stiff and dead, atop his office table. A man sat in a chair nearby — Joel Sims.

CHAPTER
SEVEN

For a while Yakima didn't know what to do. Then he remembered the light burning in the upstairs window — that would be Leona's room. He climbed the stairs. Leona's door was closed but he could see the streak of light under it.

He went back down the stairs, and then outside. He paused and stroked the stubble on his chin. Someone moved behind him. He spun, whipping out his six-shooter.

"Hello, Yakima." It was a girl's voice.

"Miss Leona?" He put back the gun. "I see your paw . . ." He wanted to say the right thing, but the words stuck in his throat.

"Yes. He's been murdered. Somebody shot him while he sat in his office. Someone outside. I thought you'd know." Her voice was cold, emotionless. "He was killed by a Forty-One-caliber bullet."

He saw now. They were trying to lay it onto Dusty. "If you think Dusty did it, you're wrong. I've been with him all day up on the north range. He's up there some place with a lame hoss now."

She went on in the same level voice: "My brother saw him do it."

"Your step brother? Rollie? Why, he's . . ."

"He's what?"

"He's dead."

Yakima rushed on and told her everything, about riding close to the dome-shaped rock, about the voices, the two shots. "I suppose you think *I* did that!"

She didn't answer for several seconds. "No, I don't believe you did. And I don't believe that Dusty killed my father, either. There are certain things that fit together now." Strength of will kept her voice steady. "Rollie had something to tell me. He left a note saying he'd meet me by that rock. Somebody else must have read that note, too. I left it up there on my table. They probably read it after I'd gone, then beat me to the rock. He had something to tell me, and they killed him so he couldn't."

There was admirable determination in her voice and manner when she turned and strode to the house.

"Joel!"

Joel hurried out. For a second he didn't recognize Yakima. Then his hand moved for the gun at his hip, but a sharp gesture from Leona made him change his mind.

"Joel, you've been a fool all along," she said. "I guess all the Wagonhammer ranchers have been fools. When I talked with Dad this morning, he told me Dusty and Yakima were sent to the country by T. H. Hawley to find out what kind of crooked work was going on." She looked at Yakima. "Am I right in guessing you've found out?"

70

"Yes. We saw with our own eyes this afternoon. Leastwise, Dusty saw with *his* own eyes. Cibber and his outfit are making ready to blast out that glacial dam in order to turn the water from the Wagonhammer into Furnace Creek, for their Furnace Flat range."

Leona explained: "That's why Dad called the meeting tonight, but he was shot before he had a chance to speak. In fact, he was shot so he *wouldn't* have a chance to speak. And that's why those men on the north range were murdered . . . so they wouldn't have a chance to speak, and why Rollie was killed tonight . . ."

"Rollie!" exclaimed Joel.

"Yes. Rollie was shot at Bald Rock not much more than an hour ago."

Joel thought for a while. He said: "Don't be took in by a pack of lies, Miss Leona. If Rollie was murdered, well, I'd say it was this *hombre* right here which did it. And as for blowin' up the glacial dam, well, that's a little far-fetched. It would take wagonloads of dynamite."

"They've been hauling wagonloads of dynamite," she said.

Yakima walked to the window of Brant's office. He climbed the banking of the house and sighted inside through the round hole the bullet had made in the windowpane. He stepped back and asked thoughtfully: "Did you say Dusty was supposed to have ridden up here and shot?"

"Yes," she answered. "But not from here . . . from behind the barn."

"Was your paw standin' or sittin' when he was hit?"

She wasn't sure.

"He was sittin'," Joel growled.

"*Hmmm*. Mighty fine shootin' for a six-gun."

Joel admitted that it was.

"Fact is, if Jim Brant was sittin', Dusty must have arched his shot."

Joel also examined the hole where the bullet passed through the pane. He lined it up with where it struck Brant, then projected the line out into distance. The line pointed directly to the barn's hayloft door.

Without a word Joel rushed inside the house. He went to the office and commenced examining the wall back of the table. He pulled out a knife and started carving at the boards. He inserted the knife point and dug out something. He was standing there, rolling some object around in his palm when Yakima and Leona found him.

Without comment he handed the object to Leona. It was a piece of lead considerably smaller than a .41 — obviously a .30-30.

Joel turned to Yakima. "I been a fool. But apologies can wait. We can't waste time jawin' now. That posse's playin' a hunch your partner will be hangin' around the Circle Two. If he is, we'd better git ourselves that way before they toss a necktie on him."

Yakima untied his horse; Joel ran for Leona's.

"I'm going along!" she objected.

Joel waved her back. "This ain't likely to end up no gal party."

Dusty watched his partner disappear around a bend in the dry wash. He stood there for a while, holding the bridle of his lame horse, listening to the monotonous thump of the drill bit, then he mounted and made his slow way back toward the Circle 2.

The cayuse steadily became lamer. The sun dropped beyond the horizon, leaving a magnificent sunset in which every hue of red, yellow, and violet were represented, but Dusty failed to appreciate it. He stroked the cayuse's mane.

"Reckon I ought to be carryin' you, judgin' from the shape you're in," he said.

He rode through the hours of night, and the first streaks of dawn were glowing up over the Windy Ridge when he came in sight of the Circle 2. From appearances, it was deserted. Half a dozen horses were in the corrals. He guessed that Benton and his boys were still out riding with the posse.

He stopped at the lower end of the corrals where he was concealed by an overhanging clump of box elder trees. There he removed the bridle and saddle from the footsore cayuse and tossed them inside the corral. He uncoiled his lariat and caught one of the horses, saddled, rode to the gate. The gate fastened with a sliding bar. He leaned over, slid the bar, pushed the gate open with his knee.

A voice cracked: "Throw up your hands!"

The man was standing in the shadow of the corral right beside him. He recognized the voice from the night before — Sheriff Till.

Someone moved on the other side, and then a couple of shadowy forms took body in front. It was hopeless to resist, he saw that instantly. He raised his hands. The sheriff stepped over and took his guns.

"Sort of figured you'd be along here," he said, "only earlier."

"I take it I'm arrested. Mind if I ask why?"

The sheriff laughed without humor. "Guess you know plenty well without me wastin' breath explainin'."

"Sure he knows!" It was Rex Benton. He strode forward. It was light enough for Dusty to see his hard, calculating eyes. "The jig's up, dry-gulcher. There's a nice cottonwood limb down the crick a piece that will be just about right to keep your toes off the ground . . . even with a four-foot lead rope. That's how we deal with your kind here on the Wagonhammer. We provide 'em with cravats . . . lariat cravats."

"I never could abide murder," someone said in a croaking voice. Dusty was surprised to recognize Ezra Cibber. The lean old man had walked up and was looking him over with sour satisfaction. "Hanging's too good for your kind," he said.

Dusty noticed how grimly silent they were. Their silence told him better than words that the posse agreed with Benton on the score of lariat cravats. He'd been in other tight spots, but none like this. He'd always supposed he might die with his Justins on, but from a bullet rather than a rope.

He said: "You still haven't said why you intend to lynch me. I'm just a little curious is all."

Benton answered: "For murdering Jim Brant."

The words stunned him for a moment. Jim Brant murdered! "When?" he demanded.

Benton laughed. "What's the matter, dry-gulcher? Didn't you look at your watch when you pulled the trigger?"

Dusty ignored him. He glanced around at the men who faced him. "Some of you fellows are on the square. If you'll give me a chance, I'll prove what's really going on around . . ."

Benton's voice cut like a bullwhip: "We'll give you the same chance you gave Jim Brant." He commanded with a sweeping gesture. "Tie him up! We'll not listen to his yarns. There's only one thing to do with fellows of his stamp. String him up and be done with it."

Several started forward. Dusty felt an almost uncontrollable impulse to run for it. But a firm hand held his horse's bridle. Men surrounded him. There was no chance. At that second Sheriff Till took one long stride, inserting himself between Dusty and the posse. The growing morning light flashed from a gun in each of his hands.

"This is my opry, boys, and I aim to do the singin' in it. I been sheriff of Watson County for nine years, and nobody's taken a prisoner away from me yet. I don't aim they should start now. Don't misunderstand me . . . I'm in favor of dry-gulchers hangin', but, as long as I'm sheriff, it'll be done up legal."

A few seconds of stunned silence followed his words. Then Cibber wailed: "Is this the kind of a thing we pay our taxes for?"

For a ragged moment Dusty wondered if the sheriff would carry his point. The tension was snapped by a familiar voice:

"Sheriff, I'm right with you. I'm for a legal hangin' every time." It was Milk River Jordan. There he stood, thumbs hanging in wide suspenders, white whiskers revolving around his chew of tobacco. "Accordin' to my idee, a legal hangin' is more dignified, and not a whit less permanent. Let's give him a fair trial and hang him afterward."

Several of the posse laughed at Milk River's words. "Sure," somebody said. "Let's *us* give him a trial."

"He'll have a jury trial," snapped the sheriff.

But the eyes of half those present were not on the sheriff now, nor on Dusty — they were fastened on the trail down the Wagonhammer. Clear on the early morning air came the swift-beating hoofs of a horse. A few seconds and the horse and rider appeared. The animal slid to a stop and Basette leaped off. He took in the scene at a glance, paused for effect.

"There's been another killin'."

"Who?" demanded the sheriff.

"Rollie Brant. Shot out near Bald Rock." He pointed to Dusty. "This fellow's pardner shot him. A varmint called Yakima. I seen him trailin' poor Rollie, then I heard a couple of shots. I rode up and found the poor kid dead."

The sheriff's voice lashed out: "Which way did the dirty dry-gulcher go?"

Basette made a long shrugging motion with his slim shoulders. "Out of the country, I suppose. Seemed to be headed toward Bedrock station."

The sheriff jammed his two guns back in the holsters. "There, I suppose, or Split Rock. We'll ride cross-country and cut him off." He gestured to his posse. "Come on, boys, hit the leather." He seemed to have forgotten all about Dusty until he was mounted and ready to ride. Then he made an exasperated gesture. "What the devil will we do with you?"

Benton waved him on: "Go ahead. We'll guard the prisoner."

Sheriff Till gestured with his arm, and he and his riders were away in a whirl of dust. Benton watched them disappear. Then he turned, his lips curling with satisfaction. He looked around at his men, and at Dusty.

"Now we can talk this thing over calmly," he said. "First, get our prisoner off his hoss. He might get ideas."

Seven were left — Dusty, Benton, Basette, Milk River, Cibber, and three Circle 2 cowboys.

Benton went on: "Basette, I dare say a slug from one of them fancy guns of yours would about solve the problem. Man tried to escape, we shot him. Simple! Nobody could blame us for that."

Basette flipped out his right-hand gun. He seemed pleased with the task Benton had assigned to him. Murder was the kind of thing Basette liked. He poised with a fastidious motion, gun barrel vertical. The hammer went back with two deadly *clicks*. Then he brought the barrel almost level.

Dusty was standing with back against the corral. Benton's men surrounded him in a wide half circle. But his horse was still there, only three or four strides away, and beyond the horse were only two men. Scant chance he'd have escaping across the level ranch yard, but still it would be better than dying here with no more chance than a cat in a bag.

"Ready?" asked Basette.

"Go ahead," answered Benton.

But the half-breed did not immediately aim. He extended the pleasure of the moment by racking the hammer back and forth a few times. Dusty's muscles went tight, ready for the spring. There was a slight movement near the corral at Dusty's left, but all were watching Basette too intently to notice it.

The report of a .45 ripped the air. But it was not Basette's gun. Basette tossed his arms like a drowning man and sprawled loosely to the hoof-trodden earth.

Benton's hands streaked for his six-guns, but a gesture from Milk River Jordan froze the motion. Milk River looked slowly from one man to the next while he thoughtfully masticated his tobacco. A wisp of bluish smoke strung up from the black muzzle of his hefty Colt.

"Now wasn't that downright outrageous of me, shootin' down that pore lad? Dusty, don't stand thar like a putrified Injun . . . select yourself some weppings. The boys will be glad to divvy up. Collect 'em all and I'll be a heap more comfortable." He evidently thought some explanation for his acts was necessary, so he went on: "You see, I'm a powerful religious man, and I just discovered that commandment number eleven reads . . . . Thou sha'n't shoot in the back." Nope, back-shootin' ain't my style. I can't tolerate it nohow, and the amount that's took place hereabouts of late has been too much for my indigestion."

Milk River's eyes shifted to the trail in the direction of Brant's. He listened. In a few seconds they all heard it — the growing rumble of many hoofs. In half a minute the posse swung in sight down the creek. A few seconds more and it was near enough to tell that Joel, Yakima, and Leona were riding in the lead with the sheriff.

"Come to think of it, I ain't kept very honorable associates lately," Milk River mumbled with alarm. He hurriedly frisked Cibber's pockets, ending up with a generous handful of gold pieces. "As I recollect, Cibber, you owe me a little matter of fifty-two dollars for haulin' that blackjack eatin' tobacco. This should about cover it, what with the interest and all." He mounted the hoss that Dusty had ready and waiting. "Well, Cibber, it's been fine workin' for you. I hope you enjoy your next home . . . the one with the Pittsburgh windows. When you get out, look me up. I know an A-rab that's hankerin' to bring in a trail herd of camels. They ought to be just the thing for your Furnace Flat range."

Milk River cracked his horse sharply and disappeared up the trail just as the posse galloped across the yard.

Cibber started to wail: "I'm innocent! I didn't know what these men were until it was too late. I'll testify against them. Basette murdered Brant and Rollie. Benton had a whip over Rollie because Rollie had been running his own father's brand to get money to gamble in Dry River. But he was afraid Rollie would squeal . . ."

In ten minutes the excitement was over. Cibber still wailed for justice, but Benton's lips only curled in an angry, frustrated snarl.

Yakima put back his gun and relaxed. He said: "Well, Dusty, it looks like everything is cleared up proper. All you need to do now is take over the peaceful job of bein' foreman of the Circle Two. Our manager seems to have resigned, so maybe you'll take his job, too."

But Dusty didn't answer. He stood with Leona, and neither seemed to hear a word.

Joel discreetly tapped Yakima's elbow. "Have you ever watched the sun rise over the Windy Ridge?" he asked.

Yakima sighed. "Awful what can happen to a good cowpoke, ain't it?" He doffed his Stetson and ran a reflective hand across his shiny dome. Then he glanced at his palm and his eyes filled with dismay. There, curling across his fingers, lay a long, red hair.

"Thunder! Another one gone. If I run into one more week like this'n, I'll be clean bald-headed."

Boothill Loves a Pilgrim

Boothill Gives a Rhythm

They forked the horses without drawing a shot. It was cool and unbelievably quiet riding the badland wash after the lines of Diehard.

"Dear me!" Waney chuckled as they climbed toward hummock. "Wouldn't the fellows back at the office have been surprised if they had seen me tonight?"

The herd was drawn in, bedded down, and a coupl of the boys were riding the long circle, singing to the rhythmic beat of their horses' hoofs. The rest were under tarps near the sagebrush fire, asleep. At one side in the privacy of the chuck wagon shadow, was a little teepee tent where I truly slept.

"Yippie-e-of It's mawnin'!" shouted Cole through cupped hands.

The boys rolled out, grumbling and looking for the dawn. Lennie emerged from her tent, winding her long hair into a knot beneath her sombrero. The light from the dying fire fell on her face, revealing the worried wrinkle between her eyebrows. She evidently suspected something was wrong.

"Trig!" she said, catching hold of Cole's stirrup. "What is it?"

CHAPTER
ONE

Little Mr. Watney, for twenty-one years assistant bookkeeper for T. Watson Beckstormer Co., Chicago, shook some of the cramp from his shoulders while he stole a look at the clock. While he was doing this, the hall door swung suddenly open, and T. Watson Beckstormer himself strode through the office.

Mr. Watney bent over his ledger and worked furiously until the boss was inside his private office.

"Whew!" said Mr. Watney. "That was a close one. Yes, indeed!"

Mr. Watney was still working at top speed when a post office messenger came in and stopped at the desk of Miss Prentice, the reception clerk.

"Have you a Mister Watney?" he asked.

Work in the office abruptly ceased. Even Will Nessling, head bookkeeper, stared through the window of his cage. This was the first time that anyone had come in the office and asked for Mr. Watney.

But most surprised was Mr. Watney. He climbed stiffly off his high stool, wiped off his glasses, and jerked to attention.

"I'm Mister Watney," he said in a voice that trembled.

The messenger strode over, thrust out a pad and pencil. "Sign here!"

But Mr. Watney knew better than to sign anything without reading it. He looked at the blank and the words written there. It was a registered letter from Coyote Wells, Montana. He had never heard of Coyote Wells. Even Montana was just a pink area on the big wall map where Beckstormer kept track of his accounts. Mr. Watney shook his head.

"There must be some mistake."

"Are you Harvey T. Watney of T. Watson Beckstormer Company, Chicago?"

"Yes, I am."

"Then it's your letter. Sign here!"

Mr. Watney signed. He took the letter, but as he had heard of certain confidence schemes whereby letters such as this were received from Spanish prisoners, he recognized the need for caution. He didn't open it right away. He carried it back to his high stool and sat there, looking at it.

Reggie Beck, the office cut-up, quipped: "Well, Watney, should we call the board of health and have it fumigated?"

Mr. Watney looked around and noticed that everyone was watching him. With trembling fingers he tore open the envelope and drew out the letter. It was written with stub pen, ornately flourished, and frequently blotted.

84

Coyote Wells, Montana Territory
June 1, 1880

Mr. H. Watney
Dear Sir:
Some time ago, your uncle, Jim Watney, appeared before me designating you his sole heir, and hence it now becomes my painful duty to tell you that the aforesaid Jim Watney passed away peacefully on the 24th inst. Your uncle leaves 2,000 patented acres centering in Rimfire range, together with chattels, appurtenances, etc. Trusting an early answer, I am,

> Your obed. serv.,
> Judge Thaddeus T. Mullens

P.S. The bullet lodged in the lower lobe of the left lung and your uncle lingered in a semi-conscious state for some time.

> T.M.

P.P.S. If you want that ranch, you'd better get here quick.

> T.M.

"Well, did your long-lost uncle leave you the old homestead?" chirped Reggie.

The question startled Mr. Watney. "Why, that's just what happened. Yes, indeed."

Mr. Watney spent some time looking at the letter, and especially at that final sentence. Then a thought

85

came to him that put goose pimples all over his back. He thought of quitting his job! This thought, combined with the mystery of that final sentence, sent a wild urge for freedom coursing through him. Mr. Watney was a bachelor. He had a little money saved. The West called. Why not?

Acting quickly before the decision burned out of him, Mr. Watney put the letter in an inside pocket and strode to T. Watson Beckstormer's door. He walked in without even knocking, and five minutes later he came out feeling strangely light-headed and perhaps fifteen years younger.

The Northern Pacific flier steamed from Fargo, leaving the green Midwest behind, and with only two slim strips of steel to guide it struck boldly out across the North Dakota plains. Mr. Watney, who had never before ventured farther west than Aurora, watched with alarm the passing of his familiar fenced-in and cultivated world.

The train left Bismarck, and thenceforth the country became even more desolate. Mr. Watney stared from the smoking-car window, a vast loneliness occupying the pit of his stomach. He longed for his cozy room at Mrs. Wickert's boarding house, for the bustle of State Street, and even for his high stool at T. Watson Beckstormer's. Night saved him from the ultimate of desolation beyond Glendive on the Montana line, and the flier clattered in at the Miles City station about dawn.

Miles City! It consisted of seven stores, three barbershops, two hotels, fifty-four saloons, and a few lesser establishments scattered over 100 acres of whitish gumbo that had been pulverized to a depth of two or three inches by the hoofs of countless horses.

It seemed to be an early-rising city to Mr. Watney when he climbed off the train about 4:30a.m. He was in error. Miles City had not yet gone to bed.

Watney walked hurriedly along the plank sidewalks, hiding his apprehension at the booted, spurred, and six-gunned citizenry, keeping his eye out for some quiet, family hotel. He ended up at one called **Mrs. Quigley's Cowboy's Rest**.

"So you want a room?" shouted Mrs. Quigley, looking at Watney's stiff hat intolerantly. "The best I can do is flop you on the floor with that government horse buyer in Number Three."

Watney was distinctly uncomfortable. He cleared his throat and revolved his hard hat a couple of times in his hand. He noticed Mrs. Quigley glaring at him, high-bosomed and florid-faced. She had evidently been drinking.

"I'm . . . sorry," he said.

He looked around and noticed a short, gorilla-armed fellow with close-set, yellowish eyes who advanced from the deep shadow at one side of the lobby where he had been snoozing in a round-backed chair. He stood for a while, staring at Watney's alligator valise.

"Is your name Watney?"

"Why . . . yes."

"Any relation of Jim Watney from the Rimfire?"

"He is . . . was . . . my uncle."

Watney didn't like the looks of this fellow. He didn't like the looks of the black belt with its filled cartridge loops that sagged around his waist; he didn't like the murderous angle at which the polished revolver butt protruded from the holster of tooled leather; chiefly he didn't like the expression in the man's eyes, that bilious, gloating look, that something which said he had been sitting there, waiting for Watney's arrival. How else, Watney asked himself, would he have guessed his identity?

A peculiar, ice-water sweat broke out at the roots of Watney's hair. His stomach became a bottomless pit, his intestines seemed to be twisting around like a nest of snakes. But in spite of all that Watney faced him with the appearance of calm. He bent, hefted his valise, and walked from the door.

"Dudes!" bellowed Mrs. Quigley, watching him go. "So a bed on a good, expensive pine floor ain't good enough for him! I should shoot them dudes when they walk in the door."

Watney strode back toward the depot. He wanted to run, but he forced himself to maintain an even pace. He kept looking ahead, although he longed to see if the man with gorilla arms was following.

Five or six young men came from a saloon, jingling their spurs, their boots clomping the sidewalk. They all talked at once, filling the air with a slow, drawling speech the like of which Watney had never heard. They fell in behind him, filling the sidewalk so he could no longer tell whether he was being followed or not.

When the cowboys turned off along a side street, Watney looked around. The man with gorilla arms was gone.

He went inside the depot, trying to laugh at his apprehension. He put down his valise, and his eye fell on the place where his name was stamped in gold leaf. So that was how the man knew! He was an old acquaintance of his uncle's probably. Nothing to worry about. Nothing at all.

Watney sat down on a curved-seated bench and listened to the *clack-clack* of the telegraph key. A young man was inside, feet on the desk, spearing sardines from a can with his jack-knife. Everything seemed calm and ordinary.

"Gosh all Jerusalem!" Mr. Watney chuckled.

He almost jumped from under his derby hat when the waiting room door swung open. He expected the gorilla-armed man to walk in, but it was a tall, thin-lipped man dressed in a seedy gray suit, dusty fedora, and scuffed, patent leather shoes.

"Hi, Wells!" the telegrapher greeted him, munching crackers.

"Hello, Steve," answered the tall man. Then he spoke to Watney. "How are you, Mister Watney?"

"Very good," Watney answered, stretching the truth a little.

"I'm Wells Ryker, attorney-at-law."

They shook hands.

Ryker said: "You look just like your uncle. Younger, but you look like him. I'd have recognized you anywhere." He sighed. "Ah, your poor uncle! My dear, dear friend. I can't tell you how badly I feel."

Watney said nothing. He was on his guard.

"An outrage, sir!" Ryker went on. "Shot in cold blood. That rustler gang from Diehard did it, you know."

"But why . . . ?"

"It was that ranch of his on the Tenderfoot. It controls the upper end of Rimfire range, and they wanted your uncle to get off. But he was stubborn and tried to fight them. So one day, just as your uncle was stepping from Leckley's general store, somebody rode out of an alley and . . . *wham!*"

"Well, gee all Jerusalem!" Watney was perspiring.

"So you see, I'm very glad I ran into you before it was too late. I can see you're a reasonable man, Mister Watney. You're not the kind who would walk right into certain death. And it's unnecessary. Yes, indeed." Ryker cleared his throat and drew a legal-appearing paper from his pocket. "It just so happens I have a buyer for that ranch your uncle left to you, and, by the merest coincidence, I also have a form for bill of sale right here in my pocket."

Watney's spinal column crystallized with suspicion. "How much are you willing to pay?"

"*Ahem!* I buy for a client, Mister Tippance Blaise, a great humanitarian. Furthermore, a crusader against the bloody rule of the Diehard gang. That is why he wants the Rimfire Ranch, even though it is unsound from a business angle." Ryker chuckled. "Oh, you're a lucky man to have run into me, Mister Watney."

"Quite an accident," said Watney dryly. "How much does your Mister Blaise want to pay?"

"Six hundred dollars! Now, if you'll just affix your signature to this line . . . Wait, I'll borrow pen and ink from the agent."

"I'd like to look at the ranch first, if you don't mind."

Ryker laughed nervously, blowing his whiskey breath around. "Ranch, indeed! Two thousand acres of alkali along a dry creek stocked with prairie dogs!"

"Then why does the Diehard gang want it?"

Evidently Ryker had no good answer for this, so he paced the station waiting room a couple of times. While he was doing this, Watney looked through the smoky windowpane and saw the gorilla-armed man roosting on a hitch rack.

"Watney, for the sake of your uncle's memory, and for no other reason, I'm willing to stretch a point and offer you eight hundred."

Watney was not tempted.

"A thousand."

"No. I believe I'll have a look at the ranch."

Ryker stopped trying to act cordial. "I'll tell you this . . . you'd be better off with a thousand dollars in your kick than you would be with a Forty-Four slug in your gizzard."

"Is that a threat?" asked Watney.

"A threat?" Ryker came down suddenly, for he noticed that the agent had stopped munching crackers to listen. "Ridiculous. Well, just a friendly offer, old fellow. Hope you reconsider. If you do, contact me at the Western Hotel."

"Well now," said Watney, watching Ryker stride across the railroad sidetracks. "This *is* a problem. Yes, indeed!"

CHAPTER
TWO

Coyote Wells lay 170 miles to the northwest on the line of the narrow-gauge Wyoming & Northern. Over at the unwheeled boxcar that served as a station, Watney learned that the twice-weekly passenger train would leave at 3:00 that afternoon, but it later turned out that 3:00 was merely a goal for the Wyoming & Northern to shoot at, and it was past 6:00 when the teakettle engine staggered, whistling, from town along its wavering roadbed, pulling a train composed of an express coach, a passenger coach, three freight cars, and a caboose.

Mr. Watney was relieved to see that the gorilla-armed man — Getchell, he had learned his name was — apparently was not aboard.

He watched the drab prairie careen past until it was too dark to see, then he roosted his feet and tried to sleep. The conductor came in, lit a smoky-chimneyed bracket lamp, and walked on whistling. Across the aisle a tall cowboy stretched out his legs and slept. Watney entertained himself for a while admiring the young man's strong profile that was silhouetted against the window and noticing how the rays from the bracket lamp reflected from the stock of his pistol. Watney wondered whether he, too, should purchase a pistol.

★ ★ ★

Watney had been asleep, but he was not asleep now. He was suddenly erect, heart racing, his spinal column rigid as a pick handle. He didn't know how long he had slept, but it must have been quite a while because the oil had burned from the bracket lamp and only a dull, red glow came from its wick. The coach weaved on with its clatter of rails, and all around him men were snoring. There was no perceptible human movement, but there was something.

He turned around slowly, very slowly, and then he saw someone was standing by the back of his seat. It was Getchell.

Watney sat still, watching the shadow from the corner of his eye and thinking a great many things. For instance, he thought that the man intended to kill him. Yet he was not afraid.

The shadow moved. Something hard with a cold feel of metal was pressed against the back of Watney's neck.

"Get movin'. Back this way."

Watney stood up slowly. He turned and took a step into the aisle. The foot of the tall cowboy was stretched out, and Watney, quite casually, trod on it. The cowboy leaped awake. His sudden movement caused Getchell to move the muzzle of his gun, and simultaneously Watney dropped to hands and knees. Getchell ripped out a curse and moved back, trying to get his gun in action.

"He's trying to murder me!" shouted Watney.

The gun roared so close it seemed to shatter his eardrums, but the bullet merely tore splinters from the floor. He was conscious of a person vaulting over him. The car became a mix-up with everyone shouting at once. He tried to stand, but he tangled with someone and fell again. The conductor ran in, holding his lantern aloft. It was two or three minutes before Mr. Watney had a chance to explain, and by that time Getchell had made his escape.

"Must have jumped," yawned the conductor, and that was that.

The tall cowboy from across the aisle eased his angular frame into the seat beside Watney, dropped tobacco into a paper, and twisted up a cigarette.

"I know, just offhand, I wouldn't take y'all for the type that had that kind of enemies," he remarked in a heart-of-Texas drawl.

Sound of the man's voice and the press of his firm shoulder took some of the chill loneliness out of Watney. He considered the remark the Texan had made. By the light of the match that the Texan applied to his cigarette, Watney could see a reflection of himself in the coach window. It was a familiar reflection, yet this time it startled him — dark business suit, hard hat, boiled collar — he hadn't realized how out of place he must look in this land.

"Well, now!" Watney chuckled. "You can't always judge a man by appearances. No, indeed."

"That's true, seh," said the Texan sincerely.

Watney then felt obliged to tell his story — so he told it all. When he was through, he asked: "What do you make of it, Mister . . . ?"

"Cole. Marvin Cole, of Brirey, Texas."

Watney was a trifle surprised to find that this weather-burned, craggy-faced young man who wore his Colt revolver with such assurance owned to a name like Marvin.

"What do I make of it, Mister Watney? Why, seh, I reckon the same boys are trying to lay you out that laid out your uncle. The gorilla *hombre*, the lawyer fellow, and this Tip Blaise must be in cahoots. Seems like I've heard of this Blaise before, but not exactly in a pleasant way." Cole looked at Watney for a while with his shrewd, blue-gray eyes. "What y'all aim to do when you light in Coyote Wells?"

The day before Watney could have answered that question without hesitation. But now it made him stop and think.

"You can't just stand around and be a target, you know. You'll either have to cash in or play out your stack."

"I don't quite . . ."

"Excuse me, seh. That's poker talk. Let me put it thisaway . . . you'll either have to sell out or fight it out."

"But surely there's a law in this land?"

"I don't hanker to alarm you, Mister Watney, but I'd say that was an optimistic view."

Watney thought for a considerable time. "I suppose you are . . . ah . . . employed?"

"Me? No, seh. I was just driftin' nawth to see if Montana was as flat as Texas."

"I don't suppose you would consent to co-operate with me in this venture? Say, as foreman of the ranch?

I'll be glad to make it worth your while. A percentage . . ."

"You mean you aim to fight it out?" asked Cole, a note of admiration strong in his voice.

"I do! But, come. What am I thinking of. How can I ask you to share my danger? After all, I . . ."

"Hold on," said Cole softly. "You cain't withdraw that offer. No, seh. The offer has been made, and I aim to accept!"

It was noon the next day when the train lurched to a stop at Coyote Wells. Watney and his tall companion shook the cramps from their knees, and stood for a while on the depot platform, looking down the length of its main street, at its false-fronted buildings, warping in the white-hot sun, at its long, ramshackle hotel, at its bank with the brick veneer front.

They obtained a room at the hotel — the Grand Central — and ate thick, rare steaks at a tiny Chinese restaurant. Then they inquired for Judge Mullens, but he was nowhere around. They started back toward the hotel, and Watney drew up suddenly and stared at a man walking toward them. It was Getchell.

"That's him," muttered Watney. "Then he didn't jump from the train, after all!"

"He seems to have somethin' on his mind," drawled Cole.

"You don't suppose . . . ?"

"Suppose he's out to get you? Why, after what happened last night, I'd say that was plumb downright possible."

Watney discovered a few drops of perspiration on his upper lip that he wiped off. "Well, gee all Jerusalem!" he swore.

Cole pulled him through a set of swinging doors to the musty, cool interior of a saloon. He ordered beers, slid one over to Watney, and they stood close to the window, watching Getchell. Getchell paced up the sidewalk and back again, interested more in a barbershop across the street than in the saloon.

The screen door of the barbershop opened and slapped shut, letting out a solidly built man with graying hair. The man headed across the street, evidently to intercept a girl who had just left Tucker's general store. He did not notice Getchell.

Getchell had been leaning against a hitch post. He got himself in motion, taking a long step up to the platform sidewalk. Just as the gray-haired man was about to pass, Getchell moved over a step, rammed him with his shoulder.

The unexpected blow sent the gray man backpedaling to bump against the corner of the bank. He said something, and Getchell answered him. The next moment the man went for his six-shooter, but he was awkward about it, and Getchell had been waiting. Getchell's hand had been on the butt of his gun all the time. He merely flipped it up, he seemed to hesitate a fraction of a second for the gray man's gun to clear the holster, then he pulled the trigger. The report broke, sharp and vicious, through the hot, afternoon air. A tiny haze of white gunsmoke drifted away in the sunlight. The victim hung to the brick veneer of the bank, his gun dangling from his fingers. Then he collapsed. A girl's terrified scream, boots clomping down the street.

Getchell made no move to escape. He just stood there by the hitch rack, watching the girl as she dropped to her knees beside the body.

Watney suddenly remembered to breathe. He was dizzy and sick to his stomach. He noticed that he was standing there alone. Cole had gone outside. The swinging door was slap-slapping on its hinges behind him. He was afraid to go, but he was afraid to stay by himself. Yes, afraid was the right word, Watney had to admit. He hurried to catch up with Cole who was crossing to the bank sidewalk.

"Seh, I'm thinkin' you should keep yourself out of this," Cole spoke over his shoulder.

Watney was suddenly ashamed of the fear that showed in his face. He was angry with himself, and he flared: "This is as much my fight as it is yours!"

"Why, I suppose it is," Cole answered. He thrust a heavy object into Watney's coat pocket. It was a large-caliber double Derringer. "Don't draw that unless you aim to use it, seh."

A dozen men were crowded around the dead man when they reached the scene. A pink-skinned albino was leaning over the girl, talking to her. She thrust him back and stood up. There were tears in her eyes, and a challenge.

"I told my father you'd murder him!" she cried at Getchell who looked on with pig-like truculence.

"This ain't no place for a girl, Miss Lennie," the albino pleaded. "You come along with me to Miss

Meeny's place. We won't let Getchell do a lope before the sheriff has a go with him."

The girl was not listening. Over the heads of the crowd she could see a handsome man of massive body come from the bank and stand on the high steps, looking down. He twisted a heavy gold watch chain with one thick forefinger.

When the girl's eyes found him, he swept off his fine, pearl-gray sombrero and walked toward her. The circle fell apart to give him room. Watney heard someone mutter the name, Tip Blaise.

Blaise laid his hand on the girl's shoulder. "Miss Lennie! I can't tell you . . ."

She drew away from him. "I told Father you would murder him if he refused to sell this time."

"*I* murder him, Miss Lennie? Why, it was Getchell . . . you can't imagine that I had anything to do with this!"

She didn't answer. She just stared at him and twisted her handkerchief into a tight ball.

"Miss Lennie, listen! You know your father threatened Getchell. You know what he said just three weeks ago. Be sensible, girl. I know this is no time to argue with you, but you'll have to listen or a great injustice will be done. If I'd wanted this thing done, do you suppose I'd have chosen a spot in front of my own bank?"

Blaise made a couple more efforts to reason with her, then he gave it up and strode back up the bank stairs. A while later Watney saw him looking from the front

100

window, his thick forefinger still twisting and untwisting his watch chain.

"There comes Judge Mullens," somebody said.

Judge Mullens was a man of fifty-five or so. He wore a wrinkled black suit, a sweaty campaign hat, a white shirt that should have gone to the laundry the day before — but for all that he managed to preserve a certain eroded, range-like respectability.

When Lennie saw Judge Mullens pushing through the crowd, a relieved cry came from her throat, and in another second her arms were around his neck and her head was against his chest.

"Oh, Judge," she wept. "See what they've done. Father . . ."

"Hush, child." He patted her shoulder. "They'll pay for it, never fear. You come along with me now. You come along to Miss Meeny's." And he led her away.

A little while later the sheriff, a raw-boned man with a red mustache, swaggered up with considerable show of authority.

"So!" he said, looking at the dead man, and then over at Getchell. "So you two finally mixed it. Anybody see this shooting?"

The first man to speak up was the albino who answered to the name of Whitey.

"Andy, and Lou Sibling and me were over in front of the Spade Flush when it happened. Getchell was standin' alongside the hitch rack about where he is now, and Mace" — he gestured at the dead man — "Mace come out of the barbershop. Mace shoved Getchell out of his way, they said somethin', and the

101

next second Mace went for his gun. I guess he got his draw hung up one way or another, so Getchell got in the first shot."

The sheriff looked over at the two men Whitey had named. They nodded solemnly. "Plain self-defense, Sheriff," Sibling said.

"That's an out-and-out falsehood!"

Everyone jumped at sound of the new voice, and the surprise was even greater once the speaker was located. It was little Mr. Watney. His face was flushed, he blinked his eyes rapidly, and he was trembling. Pointing a forefinger at Whitey, he said: "That man, sir, is a liar. I watched every bit of it from that saloon window across the street, and . . ."

"Well, look who's gettin' his two-bits' worth in!" Whitey sneered. He swaggered over and looked Watney up and down. "What kind of animal is this, anyhow? Reckon the magpies must have drug him in."

"Sir, you are in league with a murderer! You and your friends were standing over there for the express purpose of being witnesses."

"Listen, tenderfoot, I don't fancy bein' called a liar by your kind." He reached out his forefinger, hooked Watney's four-in-hand tie, and flipped it out. He stepped close, thrusting Watney back on his heels. The little man didn't notice how near he was to the edge of the sidewalk. He tried to catch himself, but he fell, landing in the deep dust. Whitey jumped down after him, evidently intending to drive a boot to his head, then he stopped suddenly for Watney was struggling to draw a Derringer from his coat pocket.

Whitey's hand streaked for his holster. The crowd scattered. Watney was still jerking at the Derringer but one of his hammers was hooked in his pocket lining. A gunshot rocked the air, but from an unexpected direction. The impact of the bullet spun Whitey half around. His gun fell to the dust. He stood for a moment, staring numbly at his shattered right forearm. He turned to locate the man who had winged him.

"You!" he gasped when he saw Marvin Cole's smoking gun still in his hand.

"Yes." Cole smiled. "I thought y'all would be some amazed to see me."

Whitey squeezed his forearm to slow the bleeding. He didn't say any more to Cole than that first word. He turned and wailed to the sheriff. "Arrest that man! Don't stand there like a damned fool. Don't you know who that man is? That's Trigger Cole! Trigger Cole, do you hear me?"

"I heard you," chewed the sheriff, looking at Cole apprehensively.

"Arrest him!"

"Reckon I can run my office without your help. You get that arm wrapped up. A couple of you boys lend a hand with Mace. Everybody that seen the killin' be at the jail in a half hour." He turned to Cole. "And you! I don't mind tellin' you that Coyote Wells is a mighty unhealthy place to keep up a reputation in."

Trigger Cole smiled politely. "Thank you for the information."

CHAPTER
THREE

The lobby of the Grand Central was cool and dark even on a day like this when heat lay in a lifeless layer close to the ground. Watney and Cole walked in and found chairs from which they could watch both the lobby and the street in front.

After an extended silence, Watney spoke: "Ah, Mister Cole, you aren't really this . . ." Watney bogged down.

"Seh?"

"You aren't really this Trigger person Whitey was talking about?"

"Now don't tell me folks talk about me 'way over in Chicago!"

"No, but by the way he spoke, and by the way those others acted . . ."

"It made you think I ate men for breakfast when I didn't have hog meat handy." Cole looked thoughtfully out from the window. "Mister Watney, do you recollect the things you thought about when you were stretched out beneath that hitch rack?" He let Watney ponder for a while before he went on. "Whitey, he was mean. He aimed to boot you, recollect? But shucks! A kick or two alongside the head don't hurt half so much as goin' to a dentist, now, does it? No, seh, it wasn't the hurt that bothered you. It was them folks a-watchin'. It was your pride that really got to painin' you. That's why y'all went for your gun, Mister Watney."

"Yes, by George, that's true!"

"That's how it was with me, seh. I was a button, you see, and sort of wild. Carried a pistol just like a sure-enough man. I didn't aim to kill anybody with it, but I practiced with it a heap just because it seemed like the thing to do. Then one night a man got to trampin' on my pride. Maybe the other man's pride hurt him, too. Maybe I was just another notch to carve on his pistol butt. Anyhow, the way it turned out, I was a bit faster at gettin' a shot in. That's why I'm around today, and that other man ain't. Well, Mister Watney, to make a long story short, that man had some friends, and by the time they was done with me, I had what the sheriff today referred to as a reputation, and I been tryin' to get away from it ever since. But there's one thing I've found out about reputations, Mister Watney. They're a whole heap easier to get than to get rid of."

That afternoon, Doc Burkie, veterinarian and coroner, held an inquest over Mace. It was established that Mace and Getchell had had trouble in the past. Lennie, Watney, and Cole all testified, but a dozen fixed witnesses swore it was Mace who started it. The jury called it self-defense, and retired to the nearest barroom.

Watney was thoughtful all the way back to the hotel. He asked: "Is your Western justice always as lenient as this?"

"Why, yes, more or less, though I'd say it was a trifle more than less here in Coyote Wells."

That night Watney slept behind a bolted door with the Derringer beneath his pillow, but nobody tried to murder him. Next day a good portion of the town turned out for Mace's funeral. Jake Lipley, the local blacksmith, conducted the simple ceremony, and Lennie was so brave through it all that Watney wanted to weep. That evening Judge Mullens came up to the room for a talk.

He mopped off his forehead with a blue bandanna and looked sharply at Watney. "Yes, you have your uncle's face, if not his size. And you have your uncle's fight, too, if I may say it."

"Was my uncle murdered by Getchell?"

"By Getchell, or one of the others. Lord, man, what difference is it who pulls the trigger? We all know the identity of the real murderer."

"Tip Blaise?"

"Of course. For five years Blaise has been reaching farther and farther, gobbling the range like an octopus. First Squawblanket Creek, then the Twentymile, now the Tenderfoot. It's water that controls the land here, you know. By the way, has he made an offer to buy you out?"

"After a fashion. He offered a thousand."

"A thousand! Your uncle's spread is worth fifty thousand. His water rights alone are worth that whether he has a head of stock or not."

"Judge Mullens . . . if you're the law . . ."

"Yes, I'm the law!" Mullens strode the tiny room a couple of times and ended by pausing to stare at himself in the little, rusty mirror over the washbowl. "I'm the law, and look at me! A lawyer at the end of his line. These frontier camps are full of us. Disbarred in the East. We drifted. This, or some other dust hole in the desert. They're all alike. And so we sit, drinking our lives out. One bottle a day, two. At last it gets us. We die. And all we leave for posterity is a heap of empty bottles."

"But you're a *judge?*"

"The term doesn't mean much here, Watney. What good is a decision with no enforcement? Blaise is the real power here, and I wouldn't last three days if I forgot it."

After Mullens left, a Chinese boy from the hotel lunchroom rapped and handed Watney a note. It was written with a bold hand on Blaise's personal stationery.

Watney penned the word — yes — across the bottom of the note and sent it back.

"Are you going to go?" asked Cole.

"I think the *two* of us had better go," Watney corrected him.

The lobby of the bank was dark when Cole and Watney climbed its high steps. "Strange," muttered Watney. "Strange, indeed."

He tried the front door. It was locked. In a moment there was a creak of someone inside, the lock bolt clattered, and the door swung open. Watney entered

107

cautiously with his right hand on the butt of his double Derringer. Cole seemed nonchalant.

"Good evenin', seh," Cole said in his habitual soft voice.

Someone standing in the shadow mumbled an answer. It was Lanagan, one of the men who had testified to self-defense the day before. He motioned to them and started down a hall, walking with cat-like tread despite the hard heels of his riding boots. He stopped before an office door beneath which glowed a streak of light. "Blaise!" he called.

There was a clomp of boots inside. The door opened abruptly, and Blaise stood, framed in the light that came from a triple bracket lamp. He bowed.

"Good evening! Mister Watney. And you, sir, Mister Cole, I believe."

The heartiness of his handshake made Watney's eyes water.

"Glad to see you, gentlemen," boomed Blaise. "Sit down! Here, Mister Watney, not that straight-backed chair. Try this one! I collect furniture, you know, and this is the joy of my heart. A little mahogany Bergère piece I picked up from a river captain. Fretted unrailing. Very rare. Chippendale."

"Very nice," said Watney. He eased himself to the edge of its cushion.

Blaise strode around behind his desk and passed out a box of cigars. Watney took one. The size of it made him seem smaller than ever.

"You, Cole?"

"Thank you, seh, I always roll my own."

Blaise sat down, creaked back in his chair, and said: "I wanted to talk about the Rimfire. Your uncle's ranch. Excuse me, Mister Watney, but as you must have guessed, I took the liberty of inquiring who you were when you arrived in town, and . . ."

"Y'all took the liberty of sendin' your man to meet him in Miles City, too, don't forget that," Cole remarked.

Blaise's eyes turned cold. "What do you mean by that?"

Cole shrugged and brushed an invisible particle of dust from the left leg of his California pants. "Why, I think it would be a good idea if you dealt the cards right out on the table."

"I don't know what you're talking about."

Watney had resolved to go easy, but with sudden anger he said: "Your lawyer, Ryker, made me an offer for the ranch in Miles City, and your Mister Getchell tried to murder me on the . . ."

"*My* man Getchell?"

Cole smiled. "Why all the play-actin'? Watney and myself know that you run things hereabouts. And we know how you do it, too. So just talk straight out, and we'll do the same. Do you agree, Watney?"

"Absolutely!"

"All right," snapped Blaise. "First of all I'll say that your uncle's ranch is not worth a damned cent more than Ryker offered you."

Watney smiled, and dropped his cigar in the cuspidor.

"However, I don't want it to stand there to be used as an outpost by that Diehard gang of rustlers. I'm willing to make a generous offer . . . four thousand dollars."

"I wouldn't sell for ten times four thousand!" Watney barked.

Blaise walked around his desk, fists doubled. He looked like a giant next to Watney. "I have ways of getting what I want!"

Watney glanced over at Cole, and sight of that calm young man gave him courage. "I won't sell!"

Blaise was known for the animal fury of his temper, and it flamed out of control now. Striking with cat-like suddenness, he drove the heel of his palm to Watney's cheek, spilling the little man backward in his chair. Cole sprang up, and Blaise spun to meet him. They faced each other for a moment, then Blaise backed around his desk. Cole stood, hunched a little, arms dangling, the palms turned a trifle out.

"I'm unarmed, you know," Blaise said.

"That is why you're still alive."

Blaise was behind his desk by now. The top drawer was open, and he rested his two hands on the table's edge, just over it. Watney stood up, shaking the dizziness from his brain. He was close to the desk, and his eyes picked up the gleam of a silver-plated six-shooter.

He shouted just as Blaise's hand moved. Cole leaped aside as Blaise's gun roared. Cole hit the floor, drawing as he went. The door to the hall was kicked open and men charged in. Cole fired, but not at Blaise who had taken refuge behind his desk. The bullet smashed the triple wick holder of the bracket lamp, blackening the room.

Guns exploded from what seemed to be every direction, lighting the room smoky red from powder flame. A sudden fury of it — then silence.

Blaise's voice: "Cover the door!"

Watney drew his Derringer. The sting of powder smoke almost strangled him, but he set his teeth and kept from coughing.

"Andy?" said a strange voice close to him.

Watney did not answer. Instead, he cocked the hammers of his double Derringer.

It was all eerie and baffling. A form sailed through the air, brushing Watney and making splinters of the rare Chippendale chair. Next thing Watney knew he was being dragged by the collar.

He tried to fire the Derringer, but then he realized he was being dragged by Cole. They reached the fresh air of the bank lobby. A little light filtered in from the saloons across the street revealing the front door and a stairway at one side.

They rushed up the stairs. A bullet thudded a board just beneath Watney's heel, and another peeled a shower of plaster by his cheek. Trigger Cole fired, the flame of his gun passing dangerously close to Watney's right ear. They found protection in an upstairs hall.

It was dark.

"Gee all Jerusalem!" cursed Watney, feeling his way along a plastered wall.

111

Cole lit a match on his thumbnail. They saw by the quick flare that the hall ran the length of the building, and then turned left. On each side were offices of veterinarians, lawyers, and quacks. Cole led the way to the end of the hall. A door opened onto a tiny verandah, and from there a stairway dropped to the street.

The town lay beneath them, and beyond that the open prairie. It was the open country that looked good to Watney, and he was three steps down the stairs when Cole grabbed him and flung him to the side of the building. He struck the building as a flame leaped from below. A bullet roared in the air by his ear. Watney fired back.

It was the first time in all his life that he had shot a gun. He'd pressed both triggers, and the recoil from the two .44 cartridges almost tore the little gun from his hand. He didn't know whether he'd hit anyone. There were two or three men down there, shooting from the corner of the bank building, and from the harness shop next to it.

Cole dragged him back to the protection of the hallway.

"Now what do we do?" wailed Watney.

Cole chuckled. "Why, seh, in cases such as this, your true Texas man reloads."

They reloaded. Watney felt a trifle better with two fresh cartridges in his Derringer, and a dozen more weighting the pockets of his coat.

Down below, Blaise could be heard shouting orders. Cole struck a match and lighted a lamp hanging at the turn of the hall.

"But . . . ," said Watney.

"The forces of evil, seh, always breed in darkness."

He went along, trying doors. He booted open one leading to a dentist's office. A window looked down on the narrow passageway between the bank and a two-story saloon building. There were Blaise men moving around down there.

"How much would you take for your ranch now, Watney?"

"Not a million dollars!" declared Watney, wishing he were back in Chicago.

Overhead, a fire hole led to the roof. Cole pointed it out, then, without saying anything, grabbed Watney by the knees and lifted him high. Held thus, the little man was able to chin himself through the opening. He reached down and gave Cole a boost.

Cole pointed across at the roof of the saloon. Between it and the bank roof was a gulf of about fourteen feet — not much for a young man, but quite a leap for Watney. It would have been out of the question altogether were it not for the fact that the saloon roof lay two or three feet lower.

"What d' you think, seh?"

Watney cleared his throat. "It takes some thinking, doesn't it?"

"Beggin' your pardon, seh, it takes a bit o' jumpin', too."

Somebody bellowed from the hall underneath: "They're on the roof!"

"Well," cried Watney, "what are we waiting for?"

Cole went first. A half dozen quick steps, and he launched himself. He seemed to float across without trying.

Watney backed almost to the far edge of the building. He crouched forward, took a deep breath, and raced across the roof. He kept his eyes, not on the abyss, but on the edge of the roof where his take-off foot should touch. Across, on the edge of the saloon, Cole crouched, ready to lend a hand. With a sudden, sinking feeling, Watney knew that he was out of step. He tried to stop, but he realized that momentum would carry him over the edge. He took a couple of quick steps. His right toe touched the edge, and the next second he was soaring through the cool night air, vaguely conscious of guns popping below. Next thing he was sprawling face down across the tar-papered roof of the saloon.

Cole dragged him to his feet. A ladder led down through a hole in the saloon roof to the second story. From there they descended a stairway to the bar.

The bar was a glare of light, but not a person was in it. Drinks and bottles stood abandoned, chip-strewn poker tables vacant with cigarettes still smoldering where they had been left. It was baffling until they realized that everybody had been called outside by the excitement.

Watney instinctively started toward the rear door, but Cole flung him around. He led the way to the green batwing doors. The front sidewalk was a press of spectators. Watney wanted to run for it, but Cole maintained a pace of exaggerated slowness.

114

It was like walking across a vast, empty stage while multitudes watched from the sides. They swung the batwing doors and strolled out, but no one gave them a glance. Everyone was craning his neck at the bank.

"Reckon it's a sure enough hold-up," a cowboy drawled.

"Hold-up nothin'," responded a white-aproned bartender. "Recollect that hard-hat shorty that blowed in with Trigger Cole? Looked pretty meek, didn't he? Know who he was? He was old Jim Watney's nephew, and he had his craw filled with revenge. Just goes to show that you can't judge a snake by the length of his rattles."

Cole and Watney crossed the platform sidewalk, descended three steps to the cinder path in front of the newspaper office, and stepped up to the sidewalk front of a general store. They were thirty or forty paces away by the time Blaise's men clomped through the empty saloon. The batwing doors flew open and flapped furiously as men rushed out and fired questions at spectators.

Cole nudged Mr. Watney, and they stepped into the shadow of a side street. The street led to a round-roofed livery stable. The night hostler stood at the door wondering what all the shooting was about. Cole went in, took a look at the stock, and pointed out a team of bays.

"Saddle 'em," he said.

The hostler recovered from his surprise. "You're loco! That's Blaise's carriage team. Brought 'em clear from Ioway, and . . ."

"Then I reckon they'll be satisfact'ry. You just tell Blaise that his friend Trigger Cole had a hankerin' for 'em."

Mention of the name was all it took. The hostler worked madly with saddles and bridles and led them to the door.

The bays twisted and side-stepped, nervous at the unaccustomed feel of saddle leather. Watney wasn't much of a rider, but he succeeded in forking one of them. The hostler kept hold of the bridles until Cole was mounted, then he turned them loose. A bronco under similar circumstances would have hit the yard sunfishing, but the high-blooded carriage team took it on the run.

Their pace satisfied Watney well indeed. The outskirt shacks and rubbish heaps of the camp flashed by, and in less than a minute the cool, sage-laden breath of the prairie was fanning his cheek.

"I'm certainly glad to be leaving that town," he said. "Yes, indeed!"

CHAPTER
FOUR

Many miles separated them from Coyote Wells by morning. They could see the town quite perfectly down across the gently dropping land. There was no sign of pursuit. No movement, save for a team and wagon that came crawling along a couple miles from town.

They rested out the noon hour in a steep-sided coulée. Watney was glad because it gave him a chance to get the saddle cramps out of his legs, and size up the country.

In time, the team and wagon came in sight over the bulge of a knoll and creaked toward them, kicking up a haze of dust with its low, metal wheels. The team didn't amount to much — just broncos — and the driver was kept busy trying to balance the doubletree. For a long time Watney thought the driver was a boy, but then a breeze came and flung out a wisp of long hair, and he recognized Lennie Mace.

Watney wondered what he should say in the way of consoling her about her father's death, but she was the one who solved that.

"I want to thank you both for coming to father's funeral," she said, pulling up the broncos and wrapping the lines around the hand brake. "It helped to know I had *two* friends there."

"You had a heap o' friends there, Miss Lennie," said Cole.

"Maybe." And the subject was changed. "You're going to take over the Rimfire?" She directed the question at Cole.

He twisted his soft Stetson and nodded seriously. "Yes'm. Mister Watney, here, has decided to fight it out. I think it's sure enough brave of him."

"Oh, fiddle-faddle!" Watney blushed.

"It's brave," she said, "but . . ."

"But crazy?" Watney nodded. "I've led a sane life for fifty-one years, Miss Mace, but I'm not going to be cheated by a gang of cut-throats."

"Do you realize what you're up against?" she asked with piercing directness.

"Reckon he has an idea after last night," drawled Cole.

"Yes, indeed!" Watney chuckled. "And maybe they have an idea what they're up against, too."

The girl didn't smile at Watney's jest.

"I don't want to scare you. It's a cinch I need friends in the country, if anyone does. But I'm going to tell you about Tip Blaise. He came here from Colorado and started the bank six years ago. It was a hard winter with an iced-over range. Cattle stacked up in the coulées and died by thousands. In the spring, Blaise was the only one left who had money to restock. That's when he got control. But Blaise didn't just stock cattle. He brought in sheep. When there was a range he wanted, he worked it over with his woolies so cattle ranchers had to move on. Some of the ranchers fought . . . but they lost. They drifted to Indian country around Milk River, and lots of them settled over at Diehard and took to rustling. Finally there were only two left . . . Jim Watney and my father."

"What d'you aim to do, Miss Lennie?" asked Cole.

"Fight it out . . . like you."

"But you're a girl!"

"Then that's my advantage."

Watney was not used to the saddle, so he rode beside Lennie in the wagon while Cole came alongside on the bay. They traveled on through the hot hours of afternoon, and toward evening they dropped to the bottom of a broad coulée where a cottonwood shack and some pole sheds were sinking into ruin.

"Driven out?" asked Watney.

Her mouth became a straight, hard line, and she answered: "It belonged to Sam Botts. Somebody poisoned the grass around his spring hole. Forty of his cows died in one day. He hanged himself right over there on the crossbar of the corral gate."

Lennie drove over to the spring and watered her team. She headed up the steep pitch leading from the coulée, and Watney looked back at the corral gate.

"Jumping Jerusalem!" he swore.

Lennie's place — the Block M — occupied broad flats on the Tenderfoot, a clear, cold stream darting with small trout. Lennie's mother had died a few years before, and, when they arrived, there was no one home except Hip Fong, the Chinese cook. Her two riders, a couple of spavined old-timers called Muggins and Arapahoe, were out riding line.

"Have trouble keepin' 'punchers?" asked Cole.

She nodded. "There aren't many willing to ride for outfits disputing water and range with Blaise. But I'm better off than the Rimfire. Jeff Pitt, the old camp cook, is the only one left there since Jim Watney was killed."

After supper, they said goodbye to Lennie and covered the remaining ten miles to the Rimfire.

Watney drew up and looked at the place spread before him in the moonlight. Like the Block M, this home ranch consisted of a log house and barn, of pole corrals, and wide meadows through which Tenderfoot Creek wound its way. A reddish light shone through one window in the house. They rode down, dismounted, and peeped inside. A baconfat lamp sat on a table, its flame casting light on a barren little room, cot at one side, harness hung on the wall, one broken-down chair with a pair of ragged, angora chaps tossed over it.

A foot stirred on the earth behind them, and they spun to find themselves staring down a gun barrel that seemed large as a train tunnel. It was a moment before Watney looked beyond the muzzle to the man who was pointing it. He was a man of sixty or so, his face gray-stubbled, his hair stringing from beneath a shapeless Tom Watson hat. The stubble revolved for a while around a chew of tobacco, then they parted and the man spoke.

"Skulkin' mighty quiet, ain't ye?"

"Ah . . . you're Jeff Pitt, I presume?" asked Watney, wishing he'd angle the pistol off to a less personal direction.

"Mebby I am."

"Well, my name is Watney. Harvey P. Watney of Chicago. I'm . . ."

"Not *you!*" Jeff stepped back and squinted from several angles. "Yep, that's the Watney nose, ding blast it." He put his old long-barreled pistol back in the band of his pants and cursed himself out of breath. "And to think I been waitin' for this! Why, I expected a ring-tailed rangy-tang like old Jim. And what do I get? A dude in a boiled hat!"

Trigger Cole took time for a good stretch and yawn. "Just a word of advice, Jeff . . . don't ever kick a boiled hat. It's likely to be filled with blastin' powder. Yes, seh! . . . it sure is."

Several weeks passed quietly. None of Blaise's gun hands came near the ranch. A couple of saddle tramps drifted in from the Musselshell where they had been riding the big circle for the 79, and Watney put them to work combing coulées for Rimfire cattle while he and Cole worked the benches. One morning they drove in a little herd of beef stock and found the usually glass-clear waters of Tenderfoot Creek gray with silt. That night the two saddle tramps drifted in with news that a dozen teams of scrapers were working at the Wrinkle place five or six miles above. Wrinkle was a squaw man, and one of Blaise's underlings.

For two weeks the water was muddy, then one morning they woke up to find only a series of pools where the creek had been. The water became warm, and the trout turned up their bellies and died. Watney spent considerable time wandering along the creek, thinking.

That night, when they were sitting around in the light of the bacon-grease dip, Watney said: "Anyway, we got upwards of seven hundred head. It's my opinion we ought to ship."

"Ship!" cackled old Jeff. "Where from?"

"From Coyote Wells, of course."

"Why do you think them steers weren't shipped last fall? A man don't hold over four-year-olds for the fun of it."

"I never considered the matter."

"I'll tell you why! Because Blaise owns a big chunk in that railroad and prevented Jim from gettin' the cars. Jim said he didn't need cars. He said he'd drive to Miles and ship on the N.P., but Blaise had an answer for that, too. He stampeded the bunch. Jim went after 'em, but they was spread across that Arrow River range. A dozen of Blaise's boys came up and stopped him. Long-geared fellow named Ratche said . . . 'Jim, if you want your cattle, you come down on the spring roundup and rep for 'em.' Jim was fightin' mad, but what could he do? He rode back home. Then this spring he sent a rep down, but he never did get more'n three-fourths of 'em."

Cole asked: "Jeff, how did Jim Watney ship before the N.P. or the W and C were built?"

"By steamboat to Kansas City. Diehard was a big shippin' point in them days."

"Then there's your answer! Let's ship from Diehard."

"Guess you ain't heard what sort of town Diehard is. She's an outlaw camp and a bad one. Even Blaise ain't big enough to ride down there and start a ruckus, much as he'd like to."

Cole smiled and twisted up a cigarette. The red flame of the grease-dip lamp lit up the strong lines of his face as he leaned forward to get a light. He settled back and blew a cloud of smoke.

"Reckon I'll drop over to this Diehard and chin some with them outlaw boys. We talk the same language, more or less."

Deep in the badlands stood the town of Diehard, a long row of warping false fronts beside the Missouri River, its population consisting of renegades, outlaws, wolfers, wood hawks for the river boats that still steamed past to Benton, and the small ranchers who had been driven from the range by Tip Blaise. It had a saloon, the Pilot House, that prophecy said would someday sink in the river silt from the lead she carried in her walls, and it had a store owned by one-eyed Jake Grubbs, the camp's self-styled mayor.

Two days after the water of Tenderfoot Creek had been shut off, Watney and Cole visited the town. It lay in a deepcut coulée with grayish clay walls, the Big Muddy rolling at its feet, peaceful in the afternoon sun despite the violent stories that were told about it. There was not a dead man on the street, or a gunshot in the air. They rode in without causing a stir of interest. The only human they could see was a broad, squat man with a tangle of black whiskers who was tilted back in a chair in front of the general store. They drew up and tied their horses to a sagging hitch rack. They saw that the man had one eye on them from the shadow of his hat — the other eye was open, too, but it was just blank white, hopelessly staring.

"Reckon you're Grubbs, the proprietor," drawled Cole.

"The same." Grubbs shot tobacco juice across the sidewalk.

"Then you're the man we came to see."

"Look me over, gents. I wouldn't be great shakes in a high-class city like Miles, but I'm plenty good for a camp like this'n. We ain't a heap particular here in Diehard."

Cole grinned. "I'm right glad to meet you, seh. I'm Marvin Cole, and yonder is my boss, Mister Watney, owner of the Rimfire."

Grubbs showed enough interest to thump forward in his chair. "Any relation of Jim Watney's?"

"My uncle."

"You don't look like him."

"I . . . I look like my mother's people."

Grubbs made a sympathetic sound in his throat. He looked at Watney and chewed for a while. "How do you get along with Blaise . . . the Coyote Wells philanthropist?"

"He tried to murder me twice. And now he's trying to break me."

"Likely do both before he's through."

"No," said Watney firmly, "I don't believe he'll do either."

Grubbs chewed for a while, looking at Watney with his shrewd eye. "Say! Maybe you look a bit like Jim Watney, after all."

Men had appeared along Diehard's street and came drifting up toward the store. They lounged around, looking at Cole and Watney. In a little while twelve or fifteen had gathered — hard-looking renegades, former cowboys, a grizzled wolfer as flea-ridden as the animals he hunted, a one-legged scoundrel who hobbled along using a .30-30 rifle for a crutch.

The one-legged one paused out in the street, reared back on his good leg, and pointed his rifle at Watney without cocking it. He said in his magpie voice: "Dog me! I ain't seen store clothes like them since I robbed that parlor train at Rocky Ridge. What you lookin' for, dude? They ain't anybody comes to Diehard for the scenery."

"Yes," said Grubbs, "what you got on your mind?"

Watney said: "We have in mind using your old loading docks. We want to ship a herd of cattle by steamboat."

"What's wrong with the railroad?"

"Tip Blaise owns it."

Grubbs chuckled. "And you want to drive your critters down here? Our reputation ain't particular good with other folks' cows, Watney."

"I'll take my chances."

The one-legged one, who they called Stumpy, hobbled up and glared at Watney suspiciously. "There's somethin' wrong with this. This is a trick. Maybe Blaise has an idea to clean us out."

One of the rustlers grinned. "Watney, there, don't look 'special like a Blaise gunman."

"No? Well, don't be fooled by a man's looks. You should have seen the Pinkerton detective that slapped me inside the Yuma pen!"

A middle-aged man with faded eyes spoke up. "Tip Blaise shot my pardner and sheeped my outfit off the range. If anybody suspects him, it ought to be me. But I can't imagine him drivin' a herd down here as part of a plan to clean us out. I say . . . let the lads load on the steamboat."

Most of the others lined up with his sentiment. This Diehard crowd did not trust Cole and Watney. They didn't trust anybody — not even one another. It was just that they were confident of their own power no matter what anybody decided to do.

After Watney set up drinks at the Pilot House, even Stumpy stopped objecting.

When they returned to the Rimfire, they met Jeff Pitt riding up from his weekly trip to the mailbox down on the stage road with a sizeable accumulation of Helena papers. Watney sat down on the kitchen step and went through them. He found out that the Chouteau County representative in the Territorial Legislature was screaming his head off for range control and that

126

Coyote Wells had been held up as the worst example of abuse.

I demand that a committee from this body visit Coyote Wells before the beef roundup, he said in one issue. In the next he added a U.S. marshal and some deputies to his demands. For two issues the legislature wrangled, and then a solid majority gave him its support.

"We're saved!" shouted Watney jubilantly, hurrying down to the corrals. "Blaise won't dare do a thing with the legislature watching him."

Cole hunkered down and read slowly through the items, while Mr. Watney jigged from one foot to the other, watching him. He laid aside the papers carefully and said: "I sure would hate to have you underrate Tip Blaise, seh. He won't quit because a committee and a couple of lawmen are on their way to look into his affairs. My guess is he'll fight all the harder to get us licked and buried before they get here. Then he can say . . . 'See, gents? We ain't havin' no trouble a-tall.' No, Mister Watney, I'd say we could expect some unpleasantness from Blaise . . . and soon."

"Dear me," said Watney.

Next day Cole saddled and rode down to see Lennie Mace. He met her riding upstream a mile from her corrals.

"I was coming to see you." She smiled, and she was beautiful, but it seemed to Cole that worry was taking some of the girlish freshness from her face. "I understand you're going to ship."

"Yes'm."

"From Diehard?"

"Word seems to get around." He wasn't surprised. News traveled fast by cayuse telegraph. Blaise probably knew, too. He had his men planted at Diehard.

She asked: "Do you think you'll get away with it?"

"With shippin' from Diehard? I don't know, Miss Lennie. But it's better than waitin' to be shot in the back."

"I started to round up a week ago."

Cole lifted his eyebrows. "How you aimin' to ship?"

"From Diehard."

"With us?"

"If I'm invited."

"You sure are," he said, smiling slowly. "Yep, you sure are!"

CHAPTER
FIVE

In a week, 2,000 head of steers and breeding stock had been grazed to the table land near Lick Springs. Jeff Pitt, who had been sent to Fort Benton, returned with word that Diamond B stern-wheelers would stop at the long disused Diehard docks in six days. The water at Lick Springs was fast disappearing, but Cole guessed the herd could hold out that long.

In the evening, Arapahoe, the spavined, old Block M cowpoke, rode back from Diehard with a caddy of Durham and some disquieting news.

"Grubbs said you'd better come down and look things over," he said to Cole. "It seems there's a one-legged *hombre* named Stumpy has fetched in some of his boys and they're plumb riled about cattle bein' driven down there. Stumpy's claimin' it's all a Blaise plot to clean 'em out."

Cole had been sprawled in front of the sagebrush fire where beans were cooking. At Arapahoe's words he got himself out to the remuda and was building himself a loop when Mr. Watney caught up.

"You can't go down there alone!"

"No?"

"No! It's not safe. You'd better take five or six men along with you."

"And get us all shot? Listen, Mister Watney, one man would be safer than a dozen. I've seen these rustler towns before."

"Well, I'm going along."

"I'd rather . . ."

"And as owner of the ranch, you can't stop me."

"Why, no, seh, Mister Watney. Put it thataway and I don't guess I can."

Darkness was gathering in the deep, badlands coulée where Diehard stood when they got there. Someone was going through the saloon, lighting hanging lamps. Grubbs's store was dark, but they could see him out in front, tilted in his chair, swatting mosquitoes.

They dismounted.

Grubbs spoke: " 'Evenin', Cole. 'Evenin', tenderfoot."

"What was y'all tellin' Arapahoe?" asked Cole.

"Just that Diehard was like dynamite on a short fuse. There's them which side with you, and them which don't. We had a bit of a shootin' over it last night. Leg wound. Personally I wish you'd never come over here with your idea of shippin' from the docks. What you aim to do?"

"To ship, of course!" said Watney.

Cole asked: "Who is it that's ringy?"

"Stumpy, Whitey Marlin, and a scar-faced fellow from down Hole-in-the-Wall way called The Dutch."

"They around now?"

"In the saloon, I reckon."

"Whitey Marlin," muttered Watney as he hurried, taking three steps to Cole's two all the way to the saloon. "Isn't that the same Whitey that . . . ?"

"He's the one."

"But he's Blaise's man."

"Yep! And I'd guess Stumpy was a Blaise man, too."

Three hanging lamps burned in the saloon. Men were gathered around a table playing stud poker. The proprietor, an unwashed fellow named Phillips, stood scowling behind the bar.

Chips rattled and there was the usual poker conversation when Cole and Mr. Watney walked through the swinging doors, but silence of a deadly, expectant quality clamped down before they were three steps inside. Watney glanced over at the poker players and was met by the pale, deadly eyes of Whitey, the albino from Coyote Wells. He sat, one hand poised, holding half a dozen white chips. The other hand, Mr. Watney noticed, was out of its sling, but a few wraps of dirty bandage still showed beneath his sun-faded shirt.

Cole ambled to the bar and roosted a boot on the rail. To Watney, who did not realize the revealing powers of mirrors, this seemed pure madness. He whispered: "Whitey's over in that game."

"Sure. I know. And Stumpy's in that chair at the end of the bar. It's like walkin' into a snake den, ain't it?"

Watney hadn't seen Stumpy. He looked to the dim end of the room, and, sure enough, there Stumpy sat, his stub leg propped up, his long, evil-looking fingers caressing the octagonal barrel of his rifle.

"Whiskey," said Cole when Phillips came up.

"The same," muttered Mr. Watney through his dry throat.

Phillips, watching with morose eyes, clumped out an unlabeled bottle. Cole poured a drink and inhaled its odor. "Don't drink it," he said to Watney.

"Is it . . . poisoned?"

"It's trade whiskey. It don't need to be."

Cole rolled out a five-dollar gold piece, and Phillips tossed it in the cash drawer.

"I'll take my change, seh," said Cole.

Phillips rubbed his palms on his hips as though drying them. His quick eyes shifted to Whitey, to Stumpy, and back again. The glance seemed to tell him something. Someone moved over at the poker table, and the squeak of his chair seemed very loud. Phillips grunted and speared four silver dollars, clanking them on the bar. Cole gathered them with his left hand and dropped them in his pocket.

Unexpectedly Cole turned and faced Whitey: "Still workin' for Tip Blaise?"

Whitey tossed down the chips in his hand and barked: "No!" He then proceeded to call Blaise some obscene names. "I'm through with him for good. He tried to dry-gulch me, so I had to hide out here."

Cole went on, speaking slowly: "I understand you been sayin' Mister Watney and me was Pinkerton men. Said we was sent down to clean out Diehard. Is it you that was sayin' them lies, Whitey?"

"You just want an excuse to kill me," Whitey whined.

"I've had that for a long time."

There was a scrape of boots on the platform sidewalk, and three strange renegades strolled in. Whitey, seeing them, took a deep breath and relaxed a little. He tossed some chips in the pot. Slowly, with measured movements, a big, raw-boned man started to deal the cards. The three renegades walked up to the bar. One of them rammed against Mr. Watney.

"Excuse me, shorty," he said, grinning lopsidedly because of a scar that ran down his left cheek to the point of his chin.

"Certainly," said Mr. Watney, moving a step away, his hand feeling by habit of the Derringer in his coat pocket.

The scar-faced fellow tossed down one shot of the trade whiskey and poured another. He nudged close to Mr. Watney.

"Drink up and have one on me, shorty."

"No thanks." Watney wanted to escape, but Cole seemed in no hurry to move. Grubbs strolled in and roosted himself on a chair to watch the poker game. Watney breathed a trifle easier. Grubbs, he felt certain, was a friend. He picked up his drink and swallowed it at one gulp. Trade whiskey or no trade whiskey, it made him feel better.

The scar-faced one looked down and grinned. He started to talk in a drawl not unlike Trigger Cole's. "Y'know, I've been on the high lope from you Pinkerton men in so many territories I could spot one of you blindfolded just by the smell. I recall one time in Abilene there was a dude came all dressed up in

Englishman's pants with one of them glass things in his eye. Y'know . . ."

"I am not a Pinkerton detective!" said Watney. He knew everyone was looking at him. To hide his nervousness he picked up the bottle of whiskey, but his hand trembled so badly he put it down again.

"You ain't?" The scar-faced man was grinning. His voice was very soft. It reminded Mr. Watney of the fur covering the claws of a cat. He nudged over a trifle closer, so his arm was against Watney's shoulder.

"Leave him alone, seh," said Cole.

The scar-faced man shrugged and poured himself another drink. "If the other folks in Diehard like Pinkerton men, who am I to raise a ruckus? I'll tell you, though, we don't cotton to 'em down in Rustler's Hole where I come from."

"Gents!" Phillips held up his hand for attention. "I've had some dealings with Pinkerton men myself, and I guess some of you other boys have had, too. There's one thing I've found out about Pinkertons . . . they always have a badge on 'em some place. Sometimes it's in the lining of their vest. Or inside a hatband. Why, the Pinkerton that nailed me after that Yellowstone stage hold-up had his badge inside the heel of his boot. Now, what I say is this . . . if the short one is on the level, maybe he wouldn't object to us lookin' him over for his badge."

Phillips waited, hands planted on the bar. Watney looked around. The room was waiting. He took a step away from the bar and nodded.

"Mister Watney, seh . . . ," started Cole, but Mr. Watney lifted his elbows defiantly.

"Go ahead and search."

Grubbs thumped forward on the front legs of his chair. As mayor of Diehard, searching suspected Pinkertons was obviously in his province, but Stumpy came from his chair, using his rifle in a grotesque gallop to head him off.

"I'll search him! And if he's a Pinkerton . . ."

Stumpy reached in Watney's right hand coat pocket and drew out the big-bore Derringer. He cackled something and put it back. He reached in Watney's vest pockets and fumbled around to the coat pocket on the other side. He snatched out something and waved it overhead.

"It's a Pinkerton badge! See for yourselves!"

Watney was stunned. Then he remembered being nudged by the scar-faced man. That was how it got into his pocket. He tried to say so, but the place was in an uproar.

"Hang him!" Stumpy was shouting. "Hang 'em both!"

Watney caught sight of Cole, backed toward the rear of the room, eyes gone cold, his gun hand hanging with that long looseness he had seen once before in Coyote Wells.

"Hold on!" barked Grubbs.

There was something about his voice that made everyone listen.

"I don't guess the little fellow had the badge on him when he came in."

135

Stumpy waved the badge and waxed furious. "You seen me take it from his pocket, didn't you? You seen me when I made . . ."

"Yep, I did. And I saw that long, scar-faced critter put it there, too."

The scar-faced man had edged away from the bar. He was crouched a trifle, his eyes like gray stone. His hands swung down, and the air of the room rocked with gunfire.

It seemed to Watney he was in the middle of it. He plunged forward to hands and knees, drawing his Derringer as he went. He had a fleeting impression of the scar-faced man, a flaming gun in each hand, and another impression of him plunging forward.

He saw Whitey twisting and weaving like a weasel in the mix-up by the card table. Stumpy had hobbled to the front door without drawing a shot. He paused there, swinging on his one leg, raising the rifle to his shoulder. The rifle was aimed at Cole. Watney pointed the Derringer and pressed both triggers. The slugs slammed Stumpy half around. His rifle discharged wildly as he went down. Watney thought he was dead, but the slugs had only stunned him. He crawled through the doors with an awkward, wild flight like a duck on land.

One of the lamps was smashed by a wild bullet. A shotgun roared, and a second light went out. Phillips was shooting with his sawed-off double-barreled from behind the bar. He got the last lamp with the second barrel, and the place went dark.

Shooting stopped. Watney sat up, fumbling to reload his Derringer, coughing from the acrid sting of powder smoke that filled the air. Men were galloping their horses away down the street. He said something, and Cole answered right by his elbow.

"There's still a varmint or two around."

Grubbs's voice came: "I got a gun in your middle, Phillips. All right, boys, let's have a light. There's a candle back of the bar."

It was half a minute before anyone could locate the candle. Its light revealed Grubbs near the back door, his long-barreled .41 pressed in Phillips's stomach.

"Never did like you, Phillips, so I can't say I was surprised to find you'd sold out your friends."

"Don't shoot!" wailed Phillips, gone sick from fear. "Blaise hired Stumpy and Whitey, I'll admit. But I didn't want to go along with 'em. They had the deadwood on me. They swore they'd take me out and turn me over to that Jackson county sheriff if I didn't . . ."

"How much did Blaise pay you?"

"Not a thing. I . . ."

A shot, a tinkle of glass, and Phillips slumped forward. He went down on all fours while Cole ran to the door. Cole fired, but the dry-gulcher was galloping his pony down the street.

"Compliments of Whitey," he said, coming back inside.

Phillips lay on the floor, his teeth clenched. Blood was running through his fingers as he held his side. "Whitey," he muttered. "That sneak. Sure I'll tell.

137

Blaise hired me. Paid three hundred. Three hundred dirty bucks. Wanted to clean out Diehard. Going to clean her out tonight. All hell will break loose . . .''

Phillips lay back, breathing heavily. One of the "rustlers", a rancher who had been sheeped out by Blaise, started bandaging the wound. After a while he stopped and felt for a heartbeat. He got up. Phillips was dead.

They carried him over beside the still form of the scar-faced man. It was silent for a moment.

"That's the start of a collection," said Grubbs.

Somebody laughed, then stopped suddenly. They all listened to the *thlot-thlot* sound of an approaching horse. The hoofs came up and slid to a halt in front of the saloon. It was Wolfer Jack, a tall, flea-bitten old sidewinder in buckskin pants and moccasins. He slid over the rump of his bareback Appaloosa horse and hurried over the sidewalk leaving the Cree bridle drag.

"They's somethin' damned sidewise goin' on in this brush," he announced. His eyes fell on the dead men and he pulled up. "Had some trouble?"

"A little," snapped Grubbs. "What was it you had on your mind?"

"Why, half a dozen lads took over my shanty, and they got every kind of gun that can be carried on a hoss. I sneaked off without 'em spottin' me. Now, if you want my opinion . . ."

He stopped short as a rattle of rifle fire broke out near a cluster of cabins up the coulée.

Grubbs said: "Must be the Stinson boys tanglin' with the Blaise gang. Likely they're comin' from yonder way,

138

too. Robertson, you sneak over to the dry wash and keep watch. Skegg, you and Idaho get out and fetch as many of the boys as hanker for Blaise hair. The rest of us better stay here. If she gets rough, I'd rather hold this old saloon than any dump in town. She's by herself, and them cottonwood logs will take plenty of lead."

A rifle made a spiteful sound from the direction of the river. There was shooting up the coulée, too, and in the direction Robertson had gone. A light wavered up and became steadily brighter.

"Guess they set fire to the old livery barn," somebody said.

The barn was an ancient, two-story structure, dehydrated by the years, and it burned like pitch shavings. An old harness shop caught a minute later, and embers flew on billowing heat waves to catch the roofs of some shacks across the street. A second fire broke out in another direction.

"That's the old Diamond G warehouse," remarked Grubbs. "Better look your last at Diehard, boys. She'll be a mite different in the mornin'."

Flames lit the front of the saloon like yellow dawn. The faces of the surrounding clay cutbanks wavered bright and dark as the fire spread. The shooting, which had died away, then broke out with concerted intensity. Watney stood by the door with his Derringer.

Cole jerked him away. "Beggin' your pardon, seh, you'd make a heap worse target here on the floor. And by the way, there's an extra Winchester that will serve for the night's work better than that Derringer you're holdin'. Let me show you some of its finer points."

Rifle slugs whined through the windows like enraged bees.

"You just move this lever down, seh, and then wheel it back up. But do it fast so the cartridge won't jam."

"The dirty cowards!" fumed Watney. "Hiding behind those burning buildings!"

"They won't be for long. The saloon here is too far away to catch, so I reckon they'll have to show themselves."

The building across the way had been a hotel. Flames roared unhampered through it as they would through a heap of dry tumbleweeds. For a few minutes it was like a great torch, then it collapsed into a pile of embers with just one skeleton wall standing. Darkness crept in again, and with it Blaise's gun hands started a cautious approach.

They came on their bellies beneath a covering fire from the coulée walls. Men crouched at every saloon window, waiting. Minute after minute passed without a pull of a trigger.

"Gosh all Jerusalem!" swore Mr. Watney who found the waiting difficult.

"Wish I'd brought my old Sharps," grumbled Wolfer Jack. "These knife-edge sights ain't within a bead of it for night shootin'."

Back in the dark Cole hummed a fragment of a range tune. Something about Sam Bass.

"What'll I do, if he dies?" asked Watney unexpectedly.

"If who dies?"

"Stumpy."

"Why, seh, in this country, it's customary to carve a notch in your gun."

The report of a rifle split the air of the saloon. Wolfer Jack chuckled with satisfaction.

"One! They's always one man that likes to show off, and there he be!"

Watney should have been sickened by such talk, but he wasn't. Instead, a burning sensation of glee rose within him. His hand tightened on the grip of the Winchester and he stared out, trying to see beyond the embers, hoping to pick out a man for himself.

A bullet tinkled some of the remaining glass in the window by Watney's cheek, and a sliver of it burned the skin of his hand. He reached to pick it out, and his eye caught a movement not thirty paces away. He aimed and brought the object into his forward sight. The gun went off, knocking Watney backward. He hadn't intended to pull the trigger just then — he'd just been squeezing too hard. He picked himself up. Someone was yelping across the way.

"Score one for the tenderfoot!" Wolfer Jack rose to congratulate Watney when something struck him. He went to the floor and lay cursing.

"Where you hit?" asked Grubbs.

"The varmints. They got my shootin' shoulder."

Jack cursed away a "rustler" who wanted to help him. He sat with his back against the wall, tearing strips from his ragged shirt for a bandage. After tying himself

141

up, he wet his trigger finger and crouched by his window.

"Wagon!" said Grubbs.

They listened. A steady rattle of wheels came from down the road.

"What . . . ?" started Watney.

Cole answered, his voice as velvet smooth as ever: "Why, they got an old wagon with the forward end planked. They'll come up the road pushin' it, I reckon, and it won't do much good to shoot at 'em."

"What'll we do?"

"Why, they'll have to stop somewhere, and, when they do, they'll have to come out from behind."

Watney peeped from the edge of the window and saw it coming, rattling and bounding at a good clip along the rough roadway. It was guided by a lariat strung from the front wheels, and the men who guided and pushed it were protected by a solid wall of planks. Shadows cast by the burning buildings showed that eight or ten men were advancing in its cover.

Wolfer Jack fired at it on general principles.

"Save your powder," said Grubbs.

The wagon rattled closely, veered a little to miss a hitch rack, smashed down an awning post, and finally stopped with one front wheel against the saloon sidewalk.

The men were so close Watney could hear their muttered exclamations and the drag of their clothing as they slid from behind the barricade. They appeared from both sides of the wagon in unison.

142

Watney fired blindly at the mass, but before he could pump another cartridge, two men drove in on him through the window. The room spun. It rocked with gunfire. Wolfer Jack was swinging his rifle, the barrel in his hands. Cole was backed to the middle of the room, his pistol pounding out streaks of flame.

It was all confusing to Watney as he staggered up. He knew he was going to die, but somehow he had ceased to care. He felt for his rifle and found it on the floor. By the light of the blazing store building he saw more men rushing the saloon. He aimed and fired, pumped and fired, again and again until the magazine was empty. The hammer fell with a barren snap, but it didn't make much difference. The men had all dug for cover.

Watney tried to stuff cartridges into the .30-30. All he had were snub-nosed .44s. Unmindful of the roaring struggle he tossed aside his rifle and loaded his Derringer.

"That's me you're swingin' your rifle at!" Grubbs roared at Wolfer Jack.

Jack stopped with his rifle in mid-air. The room was quiet. Blaise's men, those who were left, had leaped from the windows and were digging for the shadows.

Shooting slowed to an intermittent popping. The fires died down and men bound their wounds.

"Guess we fixed 'em for good that time," said the wolfer, grinning.

"Blaise don't fix up easy," growled Grubbs.

One of the "rustlers" pointed from a rear window. "There she comes!"

143

Whatever it was, he'd evidently been expecting it. It looked like a huge bonfire moving along the brow of the coulée wall. It paused for a while.

"Reckon that wagon's loaded with greasewood from the way she burns. Unless their aim's worse than I estimate, this spot's likely to get mighty warm."

With this statement of Cole's the others mutely agreed.

The wagon moved downhill, slowly, light reflecting from its tires. The fire grew as the speed of the wagon was accelerated. It hit something and turned over, and the next instant it crashed the rear of the saloon, hurling blazing faggots.

Cole flung back a man trying to get out the front door.

"They'll pick us off like prairie dogs thataway. Use the back door. Right through the fire."

One after another they went out, and Mr. Watney, pulling down his hard hat and holding his breath, went, too. There was only a moment of the flames, then he found himself against the steep dirt wall of the coulée. Trigger Cole was waiting for him.

"There's some hosses yonder," said Cole, pointing to the shadow of a little draw. "Blaise will likely head for the bench to cut the herd to pieces. It's his last fling, what with the committee and U.S. marshals and all. We better get up there and drop a word in the boys' ear. And Grubbs, you'd better bring your lads and come, too. I wouldn't say Diehard would be too healthy after the sun comes up."

CHAPTER
SIX

They forked the horses without drawing a shot. It was cool and unbelievably quiet riding the badland washes after the fires of Diehard.

"Dear me!" Watney chuckled as they climbed toward rimrock. "Wouldn't the fellows back at the office have been surprised if they had seen me tonight?"

The herd was drawn in, bedded down, and a couple of the boys were riding the long circle, singing to the rhythmic beat of their horses' hoofs. The rest were under tarps near the sagebrush fire, asleep. At one side, in the privacy of the chuck wagon shadow, was a little teepee tent where Lennie slept.

"*Yippie-i-o!* It's mawnin'!" shouted Cole through cupped hands.

The boys rolled out, grumbling and looking for the dawn. Lennie emerged from her tent, winding her long hair into a knot beneath her sombrero. The light from the dying fire fell on her face, revealing the worried wrinkle between her eyebrows. She evidently suspected something was wrong.

"Trig!" she said, catching hold of Cole's stirrup. "What is it?"

"I'd just as soon you didn't call me that, Miss Lennie. I been tryin' to get away from that Trigger business for some time."

"*Cole*, then."

"Just Marvin, if you don't mind. I like that name. It don't sound like the name of a gunman a-tall."

"Please! What's wrong?"

He thought it was her intuition. Then he noticed Wolfer Jack with his shoulder wrapped, and one of the wounded "rustlers" sagging in his saddle. It was pretty evident they had been in a fight.

"Why, I sure don't want to alarm y'all, but I'd guess Arapahoe or one of the boys should ride back to the ranch with you, Miss Lennie. We just had some shootin' business with Blaise and a batch of his gun handies, and I'd guess we was in for a bit more."

"Nobody's sending me away!" she flashed. "I'm bossing my own iron, and, if Blaise comes around here, he'll find out a Mace can shoot, too."

Cole was thoughtful. "If you put it thataway, Miss Lennie, I don't reckon there's much I can say."

Shipping from Diehard was now out of the question. There was only one move left — to drive back to the valley of the Tenderfoot.

It was a big herd and the sun was a couple hours above the horizon by the time it was moving across the wide, bench country. At mid-afternoon, Cole, who was riding point, was able to look down on the winding, green ribbon that marked the course of the stream. Eight or ten miles away were the roofs of the home ranch. In the other direction, glistening flat like

146

polished steel, was the lake backed up by Blaise's dam. From one side, a spillway ditch wound like an uncoiled snake toward a natural prairie depression that was just beginning to fill with overflow water.

Cole pointed his quirt when Watney rode up. "It would taste mighty good, that water, comin' down across the home range."

Watney nodded.

"Now, seh, if we could manage to blast that dam . . . But that requires a certain commodity known as dynamite which we ain't got." He called Wolfer Jack over. "Know where a man could pick up a couple hundred pounds of dynamite between now and tomorrow night?"

"It might be I do," said Jack, and without wasting more breath he built himself a loop and picked himself a spare horse from the remuda. By the time the herd was kicking up dirt clouds from the hill down to Tenderfoot Creek, Jack was miles away, jogging, long-legged, in the saddle toward Dry Ridge, a line of purple buttes forming the eastern border of Rimfire range.

A little muddy water lay in pools along the creekbed. It was enough for the day, and seepage might give a little more in the course of the night, and that would be the end.

"The legislators," drawled Cole, "had better get here . . . quick."

The herd bedded down that night at the home ranch. Extra guards rode circle, but everything was peaceful. In spite of his long hours without sleep, Mr. Watney spent a restless night. He was up with dawn, eating flapjacks and salt pork when he saw a puff of dust approaching along the prairie trail.

He called to Cole and pointed it out.

Cole said: "It ain't Blaise. There's only three or four men in that bunch."

Cole was right. Four horsemen swung down from the prairie trail and headed for the ranch house. In the lead was Sheriff Hank Penrose, and close on his heels were three deputies.

Penrose made his habitual movement of wiping his stringy red mustache while he looked from one man to the other. Some of them were wanted men — men from Diehard — and it made him uncomfortable.

"I got a warrant," he said bluntly.

"For whom?" asked Watney.

"For Tom Grubbs, Lester Slane, and Jim Tobin."

Slane and Tobin were two of the Diehard "rustlers". Grubbs, hearing his name, put aside a tin plate of side-pork and slouched outside, fingering his tangle of black whiskers.

"What kind of nonsense you talkin', Sheriff? What could a man o' my character be charged with?"

"With robbing the Bentville Territorial Bank."

"*Me?* Why, I'm innocent as a new-born lamb."

"Anyhow, I got a warrant." The sheriff moved around in his saddle, his eyes apprehensive. He had little relish for this task. He had no idea that Grubbs and the others would go peaceably, and it was a royal-flush cinch that he, Sheriff Hank Penrose, would not take them forcibly. It was only a play to give a semblance of

148

legality to Blaise's business, and now that he'd said his piece he was anxious to be away.

"Coming along?" he asked.

"They's twelve men here," returned Grubbs. "Reckon if you're hankern' to have me stand trial, this would be as good a place as Coyote Wells."

The sheriff muttered something, turned his horse with a jingle of bridle links, and started away. His three deputies, none of whom had uttered a word, followed him with their mounts.

"Imagine, accusin' *me* of robbin' a bank," muttered Grubbs, returning to his salt-pork. "Me, a man o' *my* reputation! Still, I'm some reliev'd he didn't bring up the subject of that Sage Creek coach."

About noon, the quiet air was startled by the rapid bark of rifle fire. Cole, who was making a trip up from the spring, put down his bucket to listen.

"That's it," he said.

"Blaise?" asked Watney.

"Blaise. This time fighting on the side of the law. It's pretty plain. The sheriff deputized the whole gang, and they're comin' down to put the sights on us for a gang of rustlers."

"Dear me," said Watney, "what will be the legislature's response to that?"

"Why, I reckon they'd side with the winners. It's always easier thataway."

Two Diehard men galloped from up the creek. The taller of them, Lester Slane, said: "Blaise with twenty. All itchin' to shoot."

A half minute later, five men came into view along the prairie rim beyond the horse corrals.

"They've split," said Cole. "Reckon he aims to get us from three ways. Grubbs, you take a couple of your best riflemen and pick yourself some roosts in the barn loft. Arapahoe, you and Max hightail it down to the lower corrals. Maybe you can keep 'em from usin' the creek bottoms for a fort. Tobin, you hold the root cellar out back . . ."

He stopped abruptly and looked at Lennie Mace. She was standing among the men, a .30-30 in the crook of her arm.

"Where do you want me?" she asked.

"Miss Lennie, I'd give eight hundred dollars, cash money, if you were a hundred miles away, but I guess that's just thinkin'."

"She's boss of the Block M," cackled Arapahoe.

Cole nodded. "And I reckon that gives her the right to shoot."

Slane started beating the glass from the windows. "I'd rather be hit by flying bullets than flying glass," he muttered.

The five riders followed rim rock for a while, then they disappeared into a dry wash. For the next ten minutes there was no movement discernible anywhere. Then a bullet whisked the air where a windowpane had been and plunked into the wall. The rifle's report arrived half a second later, and by that they knew it had been fired from long range. Another bullet followed, and another. A little puff of white smoke could be seen from among some dark rocks just beneath the rim.

150

"Reckon he's tryin' to be conspicuous," said Cole.

A few seconds later, Grubbs and his men cut loose, and answering volleys came from the deeply cut bed of the creek. It soon got too hot for Arapahoe and Max who could be seen crawling through the corrals.

After the first fury of shots, peace descended. Only a stray dozen bullets marred the quiet of afternoon. The house and barn stretched long shadows toward the creek, and the sun sank in a blaze of yellows, reds, and purples. It was every bit as excellent a sunset as Mr. Watney had viewed while crossing North Dakota, but he was in no mood to appreciate it at this particular moment.

Light hung in the sky for a long time. Twilight came, and the rifles in the barn loft started popping again. Beyond the corrals and well out of range, men were riding in a compact group. They disappeared into the brush half a mile down the winding creek.

"Reckon this is it," said Cole.

Twilight flickered. It was that time of evening between light and dark when a man's eyes play tricks on him. A cowboy aimed from the ranch house, whipping a bullet at some imagined movement between the creek and the barn.

Suddenly a rip of rifle fire broke out from the bank of an old ditch not fifty paces away. Rifles whanged from the other direction — more rifles than any of them imagined Blaise had at his command. The boys in the ranch house yipped and pumped their Winchesters until the barrels grew too hot to hold. They were tossed aside for six-shooters, but Blaise's men crept closer.

151

Watney knew the shooting was futile. Nobody could get his sights on a gun flash. "They're aiming to rush the house, aren't they?" he asked.

"Wouldn't be amazed, seh," Cole answered softly. He reached through the dark and found Lennie. She was kneeling by a window, firing a six-shooter.

"I ain't exactly the sentimental type," he said, "but I'd sure like to tell you how much I think of you."

"How much do you think of me?" she asked, her breath close against his cheek.

"Please! Don't make it any worse for me than it is. I only wish it could be different, that's all."

"Different! I think it's been . . . wonderful."

"You never can tell what'll please a woman."

He held her close for a while, and then he put her from him. He stood up, leaning against the log wall.

"A girl like you shouldn't have happened to a man named Trigger Cole," he said, a trace of the old smile in his voice. "Good women and fast pistols don't exactly go together."

Wolfer Jack rode until almost midnight, then he paused in a juniper-filled hollow near the big, barren front of Dry Ridge. Up there, he could see a mining dump, and a little to one side of this a prospector's shack. It was Charley Beek's place. Charley was a hard-rock prospector and peaceful enough, but he didn't take much to snoopers. Charley pounded high-grade in a hand mortar, got the gold out with mercury and a rocker, and stored it beneath the floor of his shack. Or so folks said. The only ones who ever investigated were two men who now lay buried some place down the hillside.

So Wolfer Jack, who was not the suicide type, rolled up in a soogan beyond rifle range and took a sleep. He got up next morning when the smoke of a sagebrush fire was coming from Beek's stovepipe, and moseyed up the hill.

"Wolfin' hereabouts?" Beek asked.

"No. I'm lookin' for the loan of two hundred pounds of Giant powder."

"What for?"

"To blow hell out of Tip Blaise."

"For that," growled Beek, "I'd spot you a ton. There's six cases of forty percent dynamite out in the dug-out. Help yourself."

Wolfer Jack diamond-hitched two of the cases on his spare horse and drifted back toward the Rimfire. He could see the flat surface of the reservoir most of the time, but it was a long way off, and it was sundown before he dropped into a coulée three or four miles away.

The evening had a fine, crystal quality, and he could hear the intermittent racket of gunfire. He found the noise reassuring, and, as twilight settled, he drifted down the coulée until he was in sight of the dam.

It was about forty feet high at the middle, filling a narrow place where the Tenderfoot did considerable winding about. The coast seemed to be clear, but Jack was not in a hurry. Folks who were in too big a hurry sometimes ended up in boothill. There was a heap of rocks above the dam where a good man with a .30-30 could make it lively, and there were some patches of buckbrush that could hide an ambusher, too. Jack hunkered down in the shade of a sand-rock boulder and scratched at some places where his fleas were itching him.

When deep dusk came, he ran down his picket rope, tightened up the cinches of his old rim-fire saddle, and headed up the crooked bottom of the creek, leading the pack horse. A gun *ka-whanged* somewhere up the draw, its bullet digging stones and sailing away with a hornet sound. Jack hadn't seen the flash, but he knew it was close. He flipped over and hit the dirt on all fours, cocking his rifle as he went. The two horses jack-rabbited up the creekbed.

He crouched there, watching the horses and cursing. They stayed close together, lead rope whipping the ground. At the base of the dam the saddle horse turned to the left, but the pack horse churned up through the unsettled earth. They hit the end of the lead rope and both of them went down.

"*E-yow!*" shouted Wolfer Jack expecting them both to be blown to glory, but the cases of powder just jumped the hitch and rolled on their corners to the bottom of the fill.

Jack crawled through earth and exposed roots as far up the cutbank side of the creek as he dared. It was almost night, but the spruce boxes were visible enough. He thoughtfully wet the forward sight of his Winchester, drew down, and let go.

The rifle's noise and recoil were lost in the roar that followed. Untamped though it was, the dynamite tore deeply into the earth fill. It sent a geyser of whitish

154

gumbo toward the sky, and the shock of its concussion opened a crack from top to bottom. In a matter of seconds the deep creekbed became a swirling torrent.

The flood roared down out of the night, thick with débris that had gathered along the creek for a century. It snatched up the pole corrals and bore them away in its first flood. Men screamed in the dark and fled before it. Its first rush parted before the high ground where house and barn sat, but a few seconds later it rose and lapped across the floors.

All shooting had stopped. Grubbs and his two men hustled in from the barn.

"The worst of her is yet to come!" he shouted. "Blaise and Whitey and that varmint Getchell sneaked into the barn, but they're welcome to it. The flood will make driftwood of her, and this house, too."

It was a pell-mell rush outside. Water rose rapidly over the sill logs. It was over Watney's shoes when he started splashing out with the rest — then he noticed the slim shadow of Trigger Cole roosted nonchalantly against the table.

"Come on, you young fool!"

"Now, seh, is that any way to talk to your chief ramrod?"

"You'll be drowned."

"I reckon I can swim out if Blaise and them others down in the barn can do it."

"But Grubbs said . . ."

"I think I'll wait around. This is Blaise's final play, and I'd like handsome well to furnish him a bit of competition."

155

"Then I'll stay, too."

"But, Lennie, she's out there, and . . ."

"That girl can take care of herself!" Then, as though Cole had disputed it: "You bet she can!"

Flood waters hung level with the windowsills, but the house stood. The barn and bunkhouse were solid, too. After reaching a crest, the flood commenced rapidly to fall. In four or five minutes the knoll lay glistening beneath a rising crescent of moon.

Cole stepped to the door to inspect the cylinder of his pistol, then, without saying a word, he started toward the barn. When Mr. Watney ran to catch up, he spun around.

"You stay here!"

"No! I'm going. If a fellow puts on a man's pants, he has to measure up to them. I'm . . ."

"Seh, stay in this door and cover me with your Winchester."

Mr. Watney knelt at the door with his rifle ready. He could see every move Cole made as he walked toward the barn. Fifty paces — it seemed an eternity. Every second Mr. Watney expected the air to be ripped by a rifle shot — but the silence held. There was only the swish of water as the creek returned to its bed, and now and then a distant shout.

Cole disappeared into the shadow of the barn, and Mr. Watney decided to breathe. There was the rattle of a homemade latch, the creak of a door opening. Silence. Half a minute of it. Then a pistol shot. Just one. Mr. Watney went a trifle sick to his stomach. He stood up, knees trembling, listening.

CHAPTER
SEVEN

Cole reached a shadow of the barn and stooped to enter the small door leading to the harness room. It was dark, the floor still puddled from the flood, the air filled with the musty odor of manure and rotting hay. He was familiar with the barn, so he had no trouble finding his way in the dark. He walked through the harness room, felt his way around a few sacks of oats, and stepped to the passage running back to the stalls.

There was a box stall at his right. He groped for its door. The door had been closed that morning, but now it was open. He stood quite still. There was silence — then one tiny sound emerged. It was the rapid *tick-tick, tick-tick* of a watch. Not the dull sound of a cowboy's dollar Ingersoll — it had the bright ring of many jewels. He knew that Blaise was waiting for him, only a step or two away.

There was a movement. It was the kind a man senses rather than sees or hears. Cole drew back as a gunshot ripped the blackness.

The burning powder brushed Cole's arm. For a fraction of a second Blaise's handsome face was revealed. He was standing inside the box stall only a stride away. There was no time, no room for Cole to draw. He drove forward, collided with Blaise, and the two smashed against the manger. The gun, batted from Blaise's hand, clumped to the floor.

Cole was lighter, less powerful, but for the moment he held the upper hand. It was a matter of timing, a matter of balance. He knew he must not let Blaise get him in his grip. It must not be made a contest of strength.

So, with the advantage still his, Cole twisted free. Blaise cursed. He flung out his mighty arms and charged forward, but Cole was not where he expected. He turned, groping. He was a hulking shadow there, against the deeper shadow of the wall. Cole could have drawn and killed him, but he didn't. He set his heels and swung a right-hand blow with all the power of his whiplash muscles.

Blaise's head snapped. He backpedaled, and slammed against the plank side of the stall. He rebounded and plunged forward to his knees.

"Blaise!" The voice belonged to Getchell, the gorilla-armed man.

Getchell struck a match and tossed it, flaring, to the floor. It revealed him as a shadow against a far wall, a hunched, long-armed shadow, grotesque. Cole knew his gorilla arms were swinging, palms open to receive the twin butts of his six-guns. The air rocked almost in unison with explosions, but Cole was one tick of a watch faster, and Getchell's two slugs rattled among the rafters of the barn. Cole's slug had drilled him a ticket to boothill.

158

Instinct told Cole that Getchell had fallen. He had no time to see for himself in the fading match light. He spun to face Blaise. Blaise had located his gun and was coming up with it. There was a movement, a quick shaft of moonlight from an opening door, and someone in another direction, too. He saw Whitey, weaving into the open, gun drawn.

No time to tangle with both men. Whipsawed. There are seconds, yes, and fifths and tenths of seconds when men live through eternities of exploding thoughts. A shot from an unexpected direction cut through Cole's momentary indecision. The bullet was not aimed at Whitey, but it startled him and threw him off. His bullet tore harmless splinters from the stall plank by Cole's cheek. He was running toward the door, and Cole let him go as he finished spinning to meet Blaise. But Blaise was slumping forward to the floor.

And then, darkness.

Watney's voice came from the harness room door. "I believe it's safe to scratch another match, Marvin."

Cole struck the match. He saw Watney there, holding his Derringer, a slight trace of smoke drifting from its right-hand barrel. On the floor Blaise had been drilled through, but he still had life in him to moan.

"Reckon you saved my life, seh," said Cole.

"It's nothing."

"It's right important to me."

"I didn't mean that. I . . . well, gosh all Jerusalem, this just about clears things up, doesn't it?"

"Yep. Whitey seems to have dusted the sagebrush, but you never quite get 'em all. It's the same with

159

rattlers. There's always one that crawls away in the rocks." Cole looked down at Blaise who was slowly reviving. "I'm right glad you decided not to kill this critter. I want to see him behind bars. Bullets are too clean, too quick for this kind. They make heroes, sometimes, when folks look back. Died with his boots on . . . it has sort of a good sound. And that ain't right. A prison suit of gray, that's what his sort deserves. It makes 'em look cheap and no-account. Yep, Mister Watney, I'm glad you aimed to wing him."

Watney cleared his throat. "Marvin."

"Seh?"

"I hate to admit this. But, the fact is, I *did* shoot to kill. Yes, indeed."

They found a bit of candle and lighted it. The door was flung open a moment later, and Lennie ran in. She saw Cole standing there, safe, and the next second her cheek was pressed against the front of his shirt.

"I'm so glad!" She wept.

Cole held her for a moment, then he stepped back, shaking his head.

"No, Lennie. You don't want me."

"I'm sorry. I thought . . ."

"Thought I cared about you? Believe me, there's nothing in the world I've wanted as much as you. A home with you, Lennie. But it can't be. Me, I'm Marvin Cole. But that's to you, and Mister Watney, yonder. To most folks I'm Trigger Cole, and the two men are a heap different. I tried to leave Trigger Cole behind, in Texas, but it was no use. He followed me to Dodge City, and from there to Cheyenne, and then

160

to Miles City, and here. Reckon he'll dog me to the end of my days. Think if you married me . . . every time I'd go to town you'd wonder if I was comin' back. I'd walk down the street, and folks would say . . . 'There's Trigger Cole.' And whenever some cheap gun slick got his snoot full of red-eye, he'd come huntin' me out, tryin' to add the big notch to his pistol. No, Lennie. I got to ride on. Maybe, if I ride far enough . . ."

Watney grabbed him, and whirled him around. "You," he said in an intense, wrathful voice, "are a damned fool!"

"Now, Mister Watney, seh . . ."

Harvey P. Watney gestured with his Derringer. "I hired you, and by heaven you're going to stay. If you try leaving here, I'll . . ."

"Put down that Derringer, seh."

"If you ride out of here, by heaven I'll shoot you from your horse. Yes, I will! Who are you that you should worry only about yourself? How about Lennie, and me? Don't we need you? You may be Trigger Cole, the gunman, but to me you're simply a coward."

"Now, seh . . ."

"Yes, a coward. Always on the run from yourself. Never willing to live down the reputation you've been saddled with."

Cole was thoughtful.

"Never looked at it just thataway," he admitted. "Nope. I never did. And maybe you're right. Maybe I better stick around for a little while." He looked at

Lennie and a slow smile spread across his face. "Maybe for a whole heap of a while."

"Well, that's more like it," said Watney, putting away his Derringer. "Yes, indeed!"

White Water Trail

CHAPTER
ONE

The steamboat *Mary Gaddes* hesitated at Cape March to take on a pilot before heading into the reef-filled waters of Tuya Inlet. Winter mist, like strips of torn gray crêpe, drifted down from the inimitable spruce forests of the Alaskan coast, and the *Mary Gaddes* moaned her whistle to warn off stray halibut trollers as she groped her way through the dishwater sea.

A short man, leaning on the rail, growled: "Why in hell didn't they build the town back on the cape?"

He wasn't actually speaking to anyone, but the tall, clean-limbed young man standing next to him answered,

"Don't blame the people who built Ketchanka. Blame the salmon. You never know what course they'll take through these islands, but they run strong along the shore farther in. That's why the canneries were built up there."

"You seem to be acquainted here."

The young man nodded. For some reason these words, intended as an opening wedge for conversation, had the opposite effect. The short man drew his lips tightly in silence as he looked across the cold sea.

165

Yes, Tim Calloway was acquainted. After four years, he was going home — to Ketchanka, scene of his family's glory, and its desolation. Especially one old acquaintance. He was going back to even a score with Brynne Keefe — King Salmon Keefe, as he was known to every Swede seiner, bohunk trap man, and gut-fingered Chinaman that made his living in the Alaskan fish business.

The forested line of Dog Island slipped past to starboard, and the *Mary Gaddes* heeled over as she swung to miss the Blunderbobs — a set of rocks over which the in-going tide rushed with a streak of white froth.

The mist strung away. A headland moved past, and Tim Calloway's pulse quickened. In a moment now he would see the red sheet-metal roof of Gallway, his father's old cannery. There would be a level stretch of coast, and five miles farther the extensive buildings of the Alaska Blue Star Company, the smaller docks of Olson Packing, and finally the town of Ketchanka lying in three terraces along the hillside.

For the moment he forgot the desire for revenge that had pulled him back to this place. He seemed to be a boy again. In his imagination he once more stood with his father on the deck of the old steam auxiliary Norcross, arriving well ahead of the supply ship to ready Gallway for the season's salmon run.

The headland moved by, and there was Gallway — the same sheet-metal roofs, the China shacks, the floating dock covered with ice. A little older, perhaps, but still the same. As the boat swung farther around the point, his eye fell on something that caused him to stiffen. There was a couple of floating fish traps, each bearing the blue and white six-point star of Alaska Blue Star, raising their criss-cross super structures from Cabbage Point.

"What's the matter, son?" asked the short man.

"Those traps with the blue stars ... they're on Calloway fishing grounds."

"Not any more, I reckon. The Calloways are gone. Old Pat's dead. That no-good son of his that quarreled with him shipped as a common sailor. You can bet King Salmon Keefe ain't the kind to let good trap locations go to waste after they're abandoned."

"That one's not abandoned."

"No?"

"No. I have it on good authority that his no-good son is on his way back to take over!"

The salmon season was still a considerable distance away, but there were enough halibut trollers tied at Ketchanka'a docks to make a considerable racket with horns and whistles when the *Mary Gaddes* came in sight and plowed the four-mile stretch of deep water to her moorings at the Northern Transportation dock.

Tim stood there, his duffel bag beside him, looking over the crowd that had gathered. They were winterers mainly, for those birds of passage, the salmon laborers, were still being rounded up from the flophouses and Chinatowns of Vancouver, Seattle, and San Francisco. There were many faces among these winterers that Tim recognized — faces from Fish Alley, from Cutler Street, and from the mansions of Nob Hill, all rubbing

167

shoulders in this single group. Brynne Keefe was not there.

In a way, Tim was relieved. Although he had had four months to think about it — all the way from Singapore to Frisco, and here — he still did not know what he would do when he met Brynne Keefe face to face. He tossed his duffel over his supple shoulder and strode down the plank.

He was lithe and strong in his movements. He was not handsome, but there was something about his square jaw, his snub nose, and his cool, sea-green eyes that made women pause and look at him — women from the line on Fish Alley, and salmon duchesses from the mansions on Nob Hill. Their eyes were on him now, but, if he noticed, he gave no sign. He walked straight on, carrying his heavy duffel bag as though it were filled with straw. He headed directly for a huge Norwegian and dropped his duffel a step or two away.

"Yah?" asked the Norseman.

"Don't you recognize me, Olaf?"

Olaf reared up straight at sound of the voice. "By golly, Aye know those Calloway voice anywhere! Tim Calloway, sure enough! Aye skal tell them damn' Blue Star seiners . . . 'You wait! Tim Calloway coom back. Maybe he have pocket full green money, too. Maybe he start up Gallway! One big year with salmon run like old day . . . one big pack, yah, and old Gallway skal show those Alaska Blue Star bloodsuckers, by yingos!' You have plenty money, yah?"

"I've got about twenty dollars."

Olaf cursed in Norwegian. "Yah, Aye bane yust damn' fool. Aye tank the old days coom back. Aye close my eyes and see Gallway seiners dump tons fish. Just like silver in summer sun. Aye see trap spiller full. Aye hear old cannery line clamp-clamp like old days, but . . ."

"I'll open Gallway, Olaf."

Olaf shook his head sadly. His huge hands, brittle and turned hard as horse's hoofs from salt water, dropped in surrender. "No. You bane young. You have big dream. But Olaf has seen! Olaf knows no broke man can beat Brynne Keefe and those damn' Blue Star people."

"My father got here broke."

"Yah."

Big Olaf said just that one word, but its meaning was plain. He did not consider Tim the equal of his father. Olaf had been his father's foreman for fifteen years. When Tim quarreled with his father, Olaf had taken the old man's part, but afterward he almost got himself fired trying to smooth it over.

"Where is he buried, Olaf?"

"Old Pat? Aye don't know. Nobody know. In those cold gray sea, Aye guess. He go out to fight those Blue Star pirate and yust never coom back."

"Is Brynne Keefe around town?"

"Yah." He reached a massive hand to Tim's shoulder. "Aye don't think you better see Brynne Keefe. Aye tank you better wait. You better tank."

"Where does he hang out?"

"You skal . . ."

169

"I asked where he hung out."

"Yah. You bane like your old father. Aye never could argue with him, neither. You know Silver Salmon Hotel? Aye guess she's built since you left. Every dinner time almost he coom down there. Brynne and his boy Tallant, and Tallant's girl, that Miss Hartman . . . by yiminy, she's pretty like anything . . ."

"Is the Silver Salmon up on Cutler Street?"

"Yah. Don't you start no trouble now . . ."

"I'll see you at the wharf tomorrow morning. We'll take a run out to Gallway."

The Silver Salmon was a two-story log structure fragrant of freshly sawed spruce. Inside, on the first floor, was one of those hotel dining and drinking rooms typical of frontier Alaska. Two men were shaking dice at a small bar in one corner of the room while the bartender, a former pug named Kid Mundt, served as referee. One of the men was a skipper of a halibut troller. He was fresh from the sea, still wearing his hip boots. The other was a small cannery operator by the name of Jack Queens.

Queens looked at Tim for a moment as though trying to recall his face. It was something of a shock when Queens failed to recognize him. Four years is not long — but in Tim's instance it was the difference between being a boy and a man.

Kid Mundt set out a bottle and glass as a matter of course. Tim tossed down a $20 gold piece, and Kid Mundt made change without taking his eyes from the dice cubes.

Tim dribbled a few drops of liquor into the glass, and stood looking around the room. There was a kitchen with a swinging door and a peephole, half a dozen tables along the far wall. In democratic frontier Alaska, such places were common domain for men and women, and for all classes.

"Brynne Keefe been around?" he asked.

Kid Mundt looked up, his eyes dull and pig-like between his big cauliflower ears. He acted like he'd just a little rather look at a man's pedigree before telling him about the great Keefe. "No," he finally answered. "But he'll be here, I suppose."

Jack Queens was looking at him again. Tim smiled to himself, wondering if the man would recognize him at all. He'd have introduced himself if it hadn't been for the others. He didn't want to advertise his arrival. It wouldn't have surprised him if Keefe owned an interest in the Silver Salmon, and this has-been pug was one of his strong boys.

"I understand Tallant's in town," remarked the halibuter.

Queens nodded. Tallant was Keefe's only son. Tim had known him as a handsome, irresponsible boy there in Ketchanka.

Tim strolled over to a table by the wall where he could watch the entire room. Jack Queens finished his dice and walked across toward Tim's chair. He was a small man, this Jack Queens, but there was something about him that indicated power.

"You're Tim Calloway," he said with a level look from his gray eyes.

"I wondered if you'd recognize me," Tim said, standing to shake hands.

"You've changed, lad. You've changed a whole hell of a lot. When you left here, you were a kid with a deck of cards where your brain should have been. But you're a man now."

"I'll try to act like one."

"Forget it . . . what I said about the cards. Hell, we all make mistakes . . . your dad as well as anyone. He wanted you awful bad after they got him crowded to the wall."

"Brynne Keefe got him, didn't he?"

Jack Queens shrugged. "Your dad knew what he was up against. Keefe had him where he wanted him and made an offer. Your dad told him to go to hell. The salmon run was poor here in the inlet, but the traps along the shore were doing well. He thought they'd pull him through, but Keefe was ahead of him. He had a dozen seiners out there pirating the fish. There was a tip came through that Keefe was going to lift that Cape Main trap, and your dad and four Swedes went out to stop him. They were never heard of again."

"And Keefe?"

"Keefe was inside this very room when it happened. Hell, lad, he hires the dirty work done for him."

"I heard they fought here in the street."

"Your dad and Keefe? Sure. They fought with their fists, but Keefe was too young. What do you plan when Keefe comes in?"

"I don't know." It was the truth. He still hadn't decided.

Queens reached beneath Tim's coat and lifted the six-shooter that he carried there in a half-breed holster. "Not this, son."

"Keefe killed my . . ."

"Draw this and you'll go out through the door feet first. They don't call him King Salmon for nothing."

There was a brittle note in Tim's voice when he asked: "What would you have me do . . . put my tail between my legs and take the next boat outside?"

"No. Not that. You can stay and fight along on a shoestring. You still have Gallway. It's as much as I have, even if it is mortgaged. Yes, I'm still running my little one-line cannery down by the Mission. Five traps, a seiner, and a tender. The run is spotty there, but I get by. I won't pretend I'm too tough for Keefe. Just too small. He hasn't bothered with me yet. I expect an offer from him this year, however."

"And then what?"

"Why, I'll take it . . ." — Queens pointed a finger at his temple and crooked his thumb like a gun hammer falling — "or else. By the way, your dad *did* will you what was left, didn't he?"

Tim nodded. He had a mortgaged cannery, a string of excellent trap sites with the traps washed away, and an old Victorian house up on Nob Hill.

Jack Queens leaned back, holding his whiskey glass with the liquor untouched, looking at Tim Calloway. He appraised his fine shoulders, his lithe waist, the strong cut of his features. He wondered about the spirit beneath. He wondered if it was the fighting spirit of old Pat Calloway — a spirit that had taken a few hundred spruce poles, some second-hand webbing, and with these had built a salmon empire equal to the Northland's best.

The room filled up as dinner time approached. Half a dozen men were at the bar. A merchant came in with his wife and daughter. They ordered dinner, and sat waiting.

There was a clatter outside the door — then a voice that sent a shock through Tim Calloway's body. It had been four years since he had heard that voice — but there was no doubting it. It was the sonorous, well-modulated voice of Brynne Keefe.

CHAPTER
TWO

Tim half rose and looked across the room beneath the gasoline hanging lamps. He expected to see Keefe come through that open door, but instead he was looking into the eyes of a girl. She was not more than twenty, yet in spite of her youth, and her slim loveliness, there was something about her, as though she had been given wisdom beyond mere years. She met Tim's eyes, and she half smiled. It was as though somewhere they had met before.

With an effort, the girl took her eyes from Tim and turned to say something to the people who followed. A tall, good-looking woman of thirty-five came in, next Tallant Keefe wearing the football emblem of the University of Washington, and after him, suave, massive and straight as one of the great cedar trees of the coastal forests — Brynne Keefe.

They walked across to a table that was set for them. Keefe paused behind the chair of the elder woman, waiting for her to drop her black fox wrap from her shoulders.

"That's Gertrude Lovillard . . . of the stage," said Queens. "Missus Keefe now. The first one divorced him, you know."

Tim nodded. He noticed that Tallant was bending over the younger woman. It irked him, although he felt no real hatred for Tallant as he did for his father.

Tim stood up.

"Take it easy, son," Queens said to him.

His action attracted the eyes of Brynne Keefe. Keefe moved suddenly in his chair. No one else had recognized Tim — but Keefe did. He stood on those mighty legs of his, and strode across the room.

"Hello, Calloway," he said.

Calloway! The name seemed to cut the air of the room, freezing conversation. The men at the bar stood with their drinks poised, staring.

Keefe did not glance to right or left. He seemed to be reading the temper of his man as he advanced. Keefe smiled, showing his strong teeth. He had personality, and dominance. It stood out now. It suddenly made Tim feel small, although he came within a half inch of Keefe's own height.

Keefe extended his hand — a powerful, well-formed hand. Like manicured steel. Tim ignored the hand and thereby, without saying a word, delivered the supreme insult of the North country.

Keefe let his hand fall to his side and paused a step away, only the slight trembling of his eyelids telling the fury that consumed him. Never, in his years in the North, had a man refused his handshake. He knew everyone there had noticed and now was wondering what he would do. A man at the bar dropped a whiskey glass. The sound of it, smashing against the rail, was like a rifle shot through the tense room. Tallant shifted

176

in his chair, smiling curiously. The girl's eyebrows were pinched in a troubled frown.

Tim Calloway spoke: "Hello, Keefe." Then, in reference to the handshake: "There's no need of being hypocritical."

"Why, that's right, Calloway. There's no use at all."

Keefe smiled a little, drawing his thin lips tightly. He shifted a trifle from one foot to the other. "You've come here looking for it, haven't you?"

Tim started to answer, but with the unexpected speed of a striking copperhead Keefe's fist lashed out. Tim had no chance to catch the blow. No chance to ride with it. The fist connected with the force of a sledge, driving him back across a chair that collapsed into a heap of twisted rungs beneath his weight.

Ordinarily a fight in the Silver Salmon would have brought Kid Mundt around the bar with his sap, but with Keefe a party to it the situation was different. Mundt merely stood there, staring.

Tim rolled over and found his way to one arm, shaking his head groggily. He made it back to his feet.

"You've had enough?" asked Keefe.

Tim did not answer. Instead, he set himself and swung a looping left. Keefe dropped his head in time to take it high on the cheek. There was a whiplash snap in the blow that rocked Keefe for a second. He recovered, set himself, and once more swung that sledge-hammer right.

Tim took it and lashed back. It was exactly what Keefe expected. He doubled, ramming Tim with his hip, pivoted, driving his elbow to the pit of Tim's stomach. The blow was devastating. It would have taken the guts out of a weaker man. There was a chance that it might have beaten Tim Calloway, but Keefe, in the supreme fury of the moment, did not wait to see. His hand flashed from the holster beneath his coat with a short-barreled, heavy revolver.

Jack Queens leaped from his chair, shouting: "He's unarmed! I have . . ."

But Keefe did not intend to shoot. He held the gun in the palm of his hand, then, while Tim was still reeling, sick from the stomach blow, Keefe drove the gun to the side of his skull.

Tim hit the floor on hands and knees. Blood oozed from the gun bruise and smeared across his cheek.

Keefe seemed to be fighting to hold himself back. Had he been in some other place he would have beaten in the skull of this pup who had insulted him, but he was in Ketchanka's best restaurant. His wife of three months was watching, so was his son, and Eva Hartman, his son's future wife. So he balanced there, but his rage was too much for him. He leaped forward.

The concussion of a gun rocked the room. It made him stop at the crest of his swing. Jack Queens was facing him with a .45-caliber revolver leveled. A little flicker of dust arose where the bullet had torn the floor.

"Put it away, Keefe," Queens said, his voice calm.

Keefe started down with the gun as though he intended to use it anyway, but Tallant ran across the room and jerked him around.

"Dad, for God's sake! Use your head. You might have killed the poor fellow."

178

Brynne Keefe trembled a moment, then he was himself again — once more the master of his emotions. "Nonsense, Son. I was merely teaching him a lesson." He turned and met the eyes of the women at his table. "Come, this is Alaska, you know."

His wife who had been Gertrude Lovillard of the stage grabbed up a bottle of cordial that had been waiting on the table and poured herself a stiff one. "Sweet Robert Fitzsimmons!" she muttered, downing it.

Eva Hartman stood beside her chair, staring at the bleeding form of Tim Calloway with fixed terror.

"Here, help me with him," Tallant said.

"You get the hell away," growled Jack Queens.

Tallant shrugged. "I was just trying to help."

"We don't need the help of any damned Keefe."

"The sins of the fathers." Tallant smiled, striding back to his table in a light-hearted manner. He said to the girl: "Why, I've always liked the bounder. Gone trouting with him a dozen times when we were kids. Say! What's the trouble, Eva? You look . . ."

"Take me home!"

"But come. This is Dad's evening. You're not going to let a little . . ."

"Take me home!"

"Take her home, Tallant," said Brynne Keefe.

Tim Calloway sat in a chair by the wall and allowed Jack Queens to swab off his slit scalp. Aside from a little, buzzing headache, he didn't feel so bad. He watched Tallant Keefe help the girl put on her wrap.

He noticed that her fingers trembled as she fastened the buttons.

"Good night, my dear," Brynne Keefe said, bowing with a slight inclination of his head.

Tim couldn't tell whether she answered him. She walked to the door with Tallant, then she paused and once more met Tim's eyes. He smiled a little, and to his surprise she gave him a smile in return.

"Eva Hartman, you say?" he asked.

"Yes. She came here with her uncle, James P. Hartman, last year. He's U.S. commissioner. Tallant came up from the States to reline his pockets out of the old man's bank account and hasn't left since. I hear it will be a June wedding."

"June," said Tim, "is a damned long way off."

"It's not too long if you're planning to put Gallway into operation."

"How about you? Are you going to sell when Keefe makes that offer?"

"I'll be damned if I will, Tim. I've been thinking it over, and I'd like mighty well to ride along with you."

"Partnership? You'd be getting the worst of it. What do I have? No cash, nothing but . . ."

"You have the finest cannery site on the coast of Alaska. You have the best trap locations. You have those, lad, through right of precedence, and the commissioner will have to protect you in it, no matter who's marrying his niece. Me . . . I have a little, one-line cannery in going condition. Neither of us could fight hard enough by ourselves to muss Keefe's hair, but together . . . well, I have lots of faith in that Calloway fighting spirit."

180

"Why, then it's a deal, Jack."

And there, beneath the eyes of Brynne Keefe, they shook hands on it.

The buildings of Gallway were long, dim, and dank. Expensive cannery machinery stood uncovered, gathering dust and corrosion. Tim spent most of next day poking around the old plant. Toward evening he went out to the floating wharf where his rowboat was tied. He was waiting for Olaf to come from his inspection of the fish elevator when he heard the *putt-putt* of a little outboard motor, and, after a moment of looking, located a boat cutting the choppy waves from the direction of Ketchanka.

The boat came straight to the float, the motor stopped, and the craft rubbed against the ice-crusted boards. He was surprised to see that the single occupant of the boat was a girl.

"I'm Eva Hartman," she said, smiling. She had been beautiful the night before, but she was even more beautiful now in her black slicker, and the sou'wester beneath which her dark hair fell in wavy profusion, sparkling with droplets of spray in the evening light.

"And I'm Tim Calloway," he answered.

"Yes, I know. I was out bounding around in my walnut shell and saw somebody over here, so I thought I'd wheel around to see who it was."

He knew well enough her coming had not been accidental, but he did not let on. There was an uncomfortable little pause. The girl stood near the edge of the float, a troubled frown gathering her eyebrows.

181

"I wanted to tell you I was sorry for what happened last night. I consider Mister Keefe's treatment of you inexcusable."

Tim shrugged. "I would have treated him the same."

"No," she said simply, "you wouldn't." Then she added: "Tallant was sorry for what happened, too."

She didn't say anything about Tallant's being her future husband, but he noticed the large, square-cut diamond solitaire on the third finger of her left hand.

"Tallant would like to be your friend," she added.

He wondered if Tallant had sent her out there. There was another pause, so he remarked: "I was just going over the old place . . . seeing whether it was all here." He pointed at the trap sites over at Cabbage Point. "I see there are a couple of Blue Star floaters on my water. Either the Keefes or myself will have to move them someday."

He said it deliberately so she would carry the word back to Tallant, but, as soon as the words had left his mouth, he knew she would say nothing to him.

"I understand those trap sites had been abandoned."

"Did your uncle tell you that?"

"Yes," she said simply.

Olaf was still not in sight, so Tim showed her through the cannery. When they came out, twilight was settling. Their ears picked up the hum of a launch motor from the direction of Blue Star village.

Eva seemed to recognize the sound of that motor. It made her nervous. A searchlight swept the edge of the float and came to rest on the two of them standing there. A gray launch came in from the gloom, water roaring in its stern as the propeller was reversed.

A tall, graceful young man hopped out. The man was Tallant Keefe.

"Eva, you devil! So you ran out on me." He turned, smiling handsomely at Tim. "Tim, old man! I should carry on the family battle, and I would if you weren't such a capital fellow."

Tallant's restless eyes sparkled while he talked. He seemed to have no hard feelings toward Tim.

"You'll never guess how I found out she followed you. The clerk at the Silver Salmon told me she came in there asking for Mister Timothy Calloway. Imagine, asking for *you*, and starting a scandal. So I put one and one together. Result . . . two. Then I came here."

Eva bit her underlip. It made her seem to be a fool after her story of just chancing to come along.

Tim said evenly: "I think Miss Hartman dislikes the idea of enmities existing. She thought maybe she could smooth it over."

She shot him a thankful glance. The explanation saved her in the eyes of both men — and, after all, it was about half true.

Tallant said: "Tim, I don't like it, either. Let me say I didn't care for Dad's treatment of you. Lord, man! The person never came north of Fifty-Four that could stand up against the fists of my father. He shouldn't have let you have it quite as hard as he did."

"You're a considerate lad, Tallant," Tim answered dryly.

"Sure. He shouldn't have bashed you like that. I'd hate to trade punches with him myself, and I dare say I'd be a match for you. I was in the national A.A.U. heavyweight semi-finals, you know." Tallant was not above spreading his feathers for Eva. He swaggered a little, for not every young man is the scion of a salmon king like Brynne Keefe. "Tim, we were always good friends in the old days. I told Eva when I kissed her good night . . ."

"Tallant!"

"Oh come, now, girl. I believe it's customary for a fellow to kiss his future wife good night."

She had not referred to her engagement to Tallant. Tim could tell that it irked her when Tallant mentioned it. He wondered why, not imagining that his own cleanly formed face and honest eyes might have anything to do with it.

Tallant went on: "Listen, now. I'm not horning in on your business, Tim. I don't know why you came here, why you were talking with Jack Queens, or why you are out looking at this rust heap tonight. But if you're planning to buck my dad and cut him out of part of this season's salmon run, for God's sakes get the idea out of your head. He's mad as a hornet already. If you try to open Gallway, he'll slap you into the sea. I tried to argue with him this morning . . . stuck up for you just for old time's sake, but it didn't do a bit of good."

"Thanks, Tallant. You're considerate. But I'll take measures for my own safety."

"Fine. I thought you'd come around to my way of thinking. Tell you what, Tim. I'll talk to him again and

184

see if I can get him to make you a good, generous offer for this cannery. After all . . ."

"Have him make it an *extremely* good offer, Tallant," Tim said, his eyes bright from the humor of the situation.

"I will. That is . . ."

"Because Gallway is *not* for sale."

"Tim, for . . ."

"And while you're talking to him, tell him to get those fish traps off my water over on Cabbage Point or he'll wake up some morning and find them riding the tide out by Cape March."

The exuberance drained from Tallant's manner. He stood, straight and handsome, looking at Tim with mingled curiosity and admiration. It was such a look as a visitor might give to a madman who showed signs of genius.

"Tim, I have to hand it to you. You have nerve. You're a fool, but you have nerve. I dread to think what's going to happen to you." He turned, laughing to himself, and held out his hand for Eva. "Come, my wandering princess. Hop aboard. We mustn't make the pater wait dinner for us."

Big Olaf came out and stood, watching as the launch pulled away.

"Aye think you bane talk too much, Tim. Now ol' Pat, he don't say nothin' he won't do, and . . ."

"You mean what I said about the traps? Hell, Olaf, you wouldn't expect me to cut them loose without warning, would you?"

"Yumpin yeehosophat!" Olaf whacked his salt-crusted pants and roared: "By yiminy, you *would* cut them trap loose. Aye tank we skal have geode fight!"

CHAPTER
THREE

A couple of days later Tim Calloway was directing a crew of winterers in their task of oil-polishing the iron chinks and other machinery at Gallway, when an Aleut came over to deliver a message. It was from James P. Hartman asking him to call that evening to discuss a matter of importance.

Tim paddled over to Ketchanka, arriving shortly before dark. He tied his skiff under the public dock and climbed the hatch that led directly to that portion of town known as Fish Alley.

Fish Alley was a double line of shacks and dives, fairly quiet now, but hell on wheels when the hordes of unruly cannery laborers arrived in the latter part of spring. Someone had mushed in from the back country with a string of malamutes that were resting on their bellies, blocking the way. Tim started to circle them, and in so doing almost ran against Tallant Keefe. Tallant had been drinking, and on his arm was one of the gals from the Red Feather honky-tonk.

Tim would have nodded and walked on, but Tallant collared him,

"Tim, you won't say anything about this if you happen to see Eva?"

"Of course not. What do you take me for?"

Tim went up the alley, past gambling houses and saloons and honky-tonks until he passed the last scattered buildings and sighted the Government House sitting on a rocky eminence surrounded by dark, pendant-branched hemlocks. He mounted the stone steps, and was shown to Hartman's office by an old Chinese in thick-soled slippers.

Hartman stood up to greet him. He was a distinguished-looking man, white-haired, with straight, thin lips.

"Calloway! I'm glad to know you. Knew your father, and I can see the family resemblance. Yes, indeed!" Hartman sat down and kept nervously opening and closing his glasses case. "Ah . . . Calloway, it has come to my attention that you are threatening to destroy certain salmon traps that are owned by Alaska Blue Star. Now, previous to my coming here, there was considerable . . . well . . . rough stuff, and . . ."

"Whoever told you I intended to destroy Blue Star property was misinformed."

"Oh?" said Hartman, lifting his eyebrows.

"Yes. It just happened that Blue Star trespassed on Gallway fishing grounds. They towed a couple of floating traps to Cabbage Point and anchored them there. I consider them abandoned property. I intend to cut them free with the tide to make room for traps of my own."

Hartman looked serious, snapping his glasses case harder than before. "Ah . . . Calloway. The way you describe your act makes little difference. Aren't you, by the act of cutting these traps free, actually destroying Alaska Blue Star property just as I said?"

Tim smiled. "I believe that is something the United States courts will have to decide."

Hartman slammed the glasses case down on his desk. "Are you threatening to carry the case over my head even before hearing my judgment on the matter?"

"Yes. Because I can tell right now what your judgment will be."

"You think I'm going to tell you Cabbage Point is Blue Star grounds through abandonment?"

"You can't, because my father fished on it last year. You are going to take the matter under advisement and investigate. While you're investigating, Blue Star will pack the Cabbage Point run."

Tim knew by the flush of anger that mounted in Hartman's face that he had guessed correctly.

"I warned you, Calloway, if you cut those traps loose . . ."

"Was that all Keefe asked you to see me about?" Tim asked, rising to go.

"Leave my office!" cried Hartman, pointing to the door with a trembling finger.

Tim nodded and stepped out just as Eva was coming down the stairs.

It was quite dark, but he could see her by the slim shadow she made. A ray of light from somewhere brought to life a needle-sharp reflection from the ring on her left hand.

"Tim! Was it about Cabbage Point?"

"Yes."

"You're angry because I told him?"

"Why should I be? I mentioned it intentionally to bring it to Keefe's attention. I don't like to strike without warning."

"You mean you thought I'd carry it to Keefe?"

"Hold on. I thought no such thing. I told it to Tallant . . . remember?"

A picture of Tallant flashed up as he had seen him a few minutes before — full of moose milk with a hussy on his arm. He felt suddenly sorry for this girl. Tallant would be a hell of a husband.

Eva walked with him to the front door. She paused there, as though she did not want him to leave so soon.

"I'm sorry I told Uncle. I thought he would see you were in the right."

"Then *you* think I'm in the right?"

"Of course I do."

They heard the *slap-slap* of Chinese slippers, and the old houseman came as far as the bend of the hall, holding a lamp aloft.

"Ho!" he said, retreating when he saw the two of them there.

He was gone, but not so quickly that Tim failed to notice the ring gone from Eva's finger.

"Why did you take off your ring?" he asked.

She moved with sudden, guilty surprise.

"The ring?"

"You had it on when you came down the stairs."

She stood very still, her head bent. Her masses of dark, waving hair fell over her shoulders. It was fragrant of salt breeze and evergreen.

190

"You didn't feel that you could wear the ring and be honest with yourself?" he asked.

"What do you mean?"

He did not answer. Instead, he reached out and closed his hands on her shoulders. She seemed almost fragile. She made no move to free herself. Suddenly, with an impulsive movement, he drew her close to him. She fought to free herself, but his strength made her efforts seem puny. He held her close for a moment, then he bent and kissed her on the lips.

A feeling of shame swept over him. He started to release her — then he realized she was not fighting against him any more. She was clinging to him, her cheek pressed against the front of his rough, woolen shirt.

She looked up and whispered his name. She pronounced it differently than before — a new meaning in her voice. The sensation of hearing it was warm and electric. He started to say something, but he heard Hartman moving around in his office. The girl started guiltily.

"Please go. If he sees, it would only cause trouble."

"Promise me one thing."

"What?"

"Promise that you won't wear that ring again."

"I promise!"

"I'll see you . . ."

"You hadn't better come here."

"But . . ."

"I'll come to you at Gallway. Tomorrow. I take a spin every day on the inlet."

He opened the door and went outside. It was frosty with a breeze coming from the great snow fields of the coastal range, but he walked all the way to the public docks before he noticed that his cap was rolled up and stuffed in his pocket.

He found Jack Queens's boat tied up beside his, so instead of going back to Gallway, he climbed the hill to the Silver Salmon. Jack Queens was there, as he expected, getting his evening exercise with the dice box.

In a few minutes Brynne Keefe came in with a stranger dressed in his Seattle clothes. Keefe passed by without glancing at Tim, escorting his guest to a private room in the rear. An hour or so passed when a rabble of excited voices sounded from the street.

The door was booted open unceremoniously, and Tallant Keefe strode in with a dozen men at his heels. The men were from Fish Alley, mostly — the type who would fasten themselves on anybody with money to spend for booze. In Tallant's case, they had evidently been promised a little excitement, too.

Tallant paused, getting his eyes used to the light. He'd been drinking enough to heighten the natural arrogance of his nature, but he was not drunk.

"Well, so *there* you are!" He walked up to Tim with a fine, muscular swing of his shoulders.

"What do you want, Tallant?"

Instead of answering the question directly, Tallant pointed to him and said: "There's the brave cannery operator! Look at him! I tried to save his hide because I felt sorry for him . . . and what did he do? He saw me coming across the street with a Venus from down in

Fish Alley, and ran right straight and told Eva Hartman about . . ."

"Don't mention Eva's name again."

The words were not spoken loudly, but they had a quality that cut like a saw through Tallant's denunciation.

"Now he tells me I can't even mention her name . . ."

"Tallant . . . ," started Kid Mundt.

"Stay back there where you belong, ears!" The Fish Alley crowd snickered at this reference to Kid Mundt's cauliflowers. "I'm going to tell this would-be cannery man what he is."

Tallant thereupon proceeded to mouth a string of vile names.

"Keep still." Tim held his temper. "I don't like to pop a drunken man."

"I'll show you how drunk I am!"

Tallant weaved swiftly forward, lashing with his left hand. He was a college athlete. He had fought with his boxing team in the Olympic eliminations, and he knew how to handle himself. But Tim had had a training of a sort, too, although his college had been the forecastle of a steam auxiliary on the Oriental run, and his opponents, recruited from the waterfronts of the world, had heard of Harvard, Yale, and Notre Dame nowhere except in the football lotteries.

So, when that left snaked out with a snap, developed by punching the light bag, Tim rode with it, countered, shifted, and came over with a right that shook Tallant's teeth. Tallant was put on his heels for a second. He tried to bob low and come up with a left hook. He made the mistake of telegraphing the move. He bent, but Tim followed him down with an overhand right.

Tallant sprawled on the floor. He reeled up, pawing with his left hand. Tim brushed it away, hesitated a fraction of a second for timing, and delivered a right-hand blow that smashed Tallant back to the floor.

He whirled in time to face Kid Mundt who was running around the end of the bar with his sap. Mundt had been a pug, although never a very good one, and he was too fat now. He saw the fist on its way as he hesitated there, his sap lifted high. He tried to retreat, but it was too late. He went down as though struck by a pike pole.

Brynne Keefe had heard the excitement in his private room. He hurried out and drew up sharply at the sight of his son sprawled cheek down among the cigar stubs on the floor. He turned and looked at Tim, his face draining of color.

"You were afraid of me, so you picked on my son?"

His voice was brittle as broken ice.

Tim answered: "Your son came here looking for it, and he found it. Why don't you take him home?"

It was evident that Keefe considered Tallant a moral weakling, so Tim took a primitive delight in saying the words that could only add to his fury.

"You're ashamed of him, aren't you?"

Keefe started forward, and then he seemed to realize that Tim was trying to egg him on and resume the battle where it had left off a few nights before.

"Why don't you have that hoodlum arrested?" asked the man in Seattle clothes, pointing to Tim.

Sound of his voice seemed to give Keefe a better grip on his emotions. He turned and helped his son who was pulling his way up from the floor.

"Where is he?" Tallant muttered. "Where is that . . . ?"

"Tallant! Not tonight. Here, take my shoulder."

Keefe turned and located Kid Mundt who wasn't feeling any too sharp, either. "Mundt . . . bring us some whiskies to the back room!"

CHAPTER
FOUR

Holgar Shenska, known throughout Alaskan fishing waters as Holgar The Horse, stood near the front window of the Gill Net Saloon and looked with dull eyes at the early spring rain that was making Fish Alley a quagmire.

The Horse had arrived in Alaskan waters nine years before, and had spent five of those years on a halibut troller, patiently doing the work of two men for one man's pay. He might have gone on in that manner to the end of his days had not Brynne Keefe chanced to see him one night in the process of wrecking one of the joints on the Alley.

A table had sailed through the front window, taking a length of frame with it, splattering glass in Keefe's face. Spangler, the Alaska Blue Star special deputy, had reached inside his Mackinaw for the butt of his ever-handy .45 and asked: "Want me to calm him down, boss?"

"Let him go," Keefe had said, smiling, and next morning he had sent Spangler around to hire The Horse at double pay. The Horse's duties were simple. He was to remain available for special tasks. Perhaps the special task was to dump a labor organizer in the bay, or to crack the jaw of some independent seiner. Whatever it was, The Horse performed as ordered.

The Horse was just turning from the window to order another mug of beer when his dull eyes fell on the familiar form of Spangler coming in boots, slicker, and sou'wester.

"Maybe I get yob," he commented, hitching up his pants.

Spangler poked his head inside the door and said: "Come along."

"Yah," answered The Horse.

He put on his oilskins and plodded along, slightly to Spangler's rear, like a trained bear following its keeper.

Spangler went to the Blue Star wharf shanty where five men were sitting around the stove.

"Where's Big Chris?" he asked a former salmon pirate named Freeland.

"Drunk," answered Freeland.

"Go get him."

Freeland grumbled and went out, buttoning a slicker over his Mackinaw. Spangler stood by the steamed-over window, looking at the vague outlines of halibut and salmon trollers tied at the docks. When he wiped the steam from the pane, he could see the dim features of Gallway, and a mile or so closer the whitish streaks that marked the positions of those two Blue Star traps at Cabbage Point. Strips of fog kept sliding in from the timbered mountains, mixing with the rain that kept whipping across the inlet.

Freeland came back with Big Chris, a Swede only fifty or sixty pounds lighter than The Horse. Chris was not drunk, but he was still shaky after a bad night.

Spangler barked at him: "Damn you, when I say nine o'clock, I mean nine o'clock!"

Big Chris hiccupped and flopped down on a bench, leaning forward with elbows on knees so that the backs of his hands almost touched the floor. He looked at Spangler as though he hated his guts, but he knew better than to say anything at the moment.

Spangler pointed from the steamy window. "Do you see those traps over on Cabbage Point?" Nobody bothered to look. "Well, Calloway has an idea he's going to cut them loose on the tide tonight, and we're going to stop him."

"How?" asked Freeland.

"We're going to be out there, four of us in each of the watchman's shanties, waiting for him."

"Aye tank you bane in a big hurry to get me har at nine o'clock," muttered Big Chris, twisting the lid from his box of snoose.

"When I want your opinion, I'll ask for it."

Freeland said: "Nobody asked for my opinion, either, but if Calloway sees us go over there, he'll know better than make a play at those traps. He's no fool, that Calloway, and he's tough. In fact, he's tougher'n hell. I don't mind earning a few fast bucks on a job like this, but I don't hanker to get caught on any ocean-going salmon trap. If he knows we're there, he'll find a way to . . ."

"If you'd shut up and listen, I'd explain it to you. Now, we know he's going to tackle them tonight. There's plenty of soupy weather blowing down from the straits, according to the dot-dash, so the inlet should be grayed out before the day's over. When it is, we'll take a couple of skiffs and get over there without anyone knowing. If the fog happens to lift so they can see us from Gallway, to hell with it . . . we'll have to figure out something else then."

"What do we do . . . fight 'em with our hands?" asked Freeland.

"There's a rifle for each of you down in the boats."

"Do we shoot to kill?"

"If I didn't want you to shoot to kill, I'd give you a pocketful of firecrackers."

There was a moment while the men listened to a piece of tar paper flapping on the roof.

"What's the penalty for murder?" asked a hard-faced fellow named Lockley.

Chris replied: "Hangin' aye tank."

Freeland chimed in: "Your damned right it's hangin'."

Spangler said: "You'll be protected. You're guards on a trap, and that gives you the right to shoot at trespassers. You don't need to be afraid with old King Salmon Keefe backing you."

They waited. The fog came in successive wind-blown sheets, but now and then a hole opened so they could see the outline of the country across the inlet.

"How the hell can you be so sure that Calloway is going after those traps tonight?" Lockley asked.

Freeland answered: "Why, Keefe has a little set of ears. The prettiest set in Ketchanka. Sure . . . Eva Hartman. She picked it up from Calloway and peddled it to the judge. Tried to get him to order the traps removed. He said he'd do it, if he knew just when Calloway planned to act. Holy bald-headed hell and she went for it! So the judge . . ."

"Shut up," muttered Spangler.

The cold, rainy mist became solid shortly before noon. When it was so thick they could barely see the end of the Blue Star docks, the men descended the rowboat hatch and set out across the inlet.

It was wet work, quartering the waves, with the wind carrying rain. Despite their slickers they were soaked by the time they reached the floating traps. Spangler with The Horse and two others took charge of the trap nearest Gallway, and he put Freeland in charge of the other, which was a half mile closer to town. They hauled their boats over the pot timbers and scooped them two-thirds full of water to prevent them being visible except from above.

The day wore away, gray and cold, with the shacks weaving in the wind.

Big Chris hunched against the wall for a couple of hours, then he stood up and commenced shaving kindling into the dinky wood stove.

"What do you think you're doing?" asked Freeland.

"Aye bane goin' to start fire."

"You'll start no fire here!"

Chris beat on the sheet-metal stove top with his fist: "Aye bane cold!"

"Start that fire, and Spangler will be over here with his six-gun and he'll warm you up."

Chris thought that over. He was afraid of Spangler, but his bout with John Barleycorn had taken his resistance down, and the wet had crawled inside his clothes.

"All right, Aye don' build fire, but Aye goin' to go back for bottle."

"You'll stay here!"

"Aye be back in plenty time. Aye bring bottle for you feller, too."

"Let him go," said a former jailbird named Demart.

This was all the encouragement Big Chris needed. He stood up, buttoning his oilskin coat, pulling his soggy Scotch cap down over his ears. The thought of whiskey brought back some of his natural cheerfulness. "Skol!" he shouted, lifting a hand as though it already contained a flagon.

"You won't leave here," snarled Freeland.

"Ho! Aye leave all right . . ."

Freeland leaped in front of him, seizing a rifle as he went. Chris hesitated a moment, standing so tall the bottom of his cap touched the deadening felt that had been nailed over the ceiling. With a swing of his fist he batted Freeland to the wall. Freeland rebounded, his rifle clattering away. Chris smashed him again, dropping him like a dead man.

"Skol," Chris muttered, looking at the huddled form of the fish pirate. "Noo skal ve go, yah!"

The wind caught him, almost whipping him from under the ladder as he descended to the squared spruce logs that made up the floating framework of the pot — that web-lined inner portion of the trap where salmon were herded by means of the long lead and an intricate system of barricades. He balanced himself on the slippery framework, his oilskins flapping in the wind as he bailed out the boat. Then he dragged the craft to open water and set out with the wind at his back for Ketchanka, six miles away.

Tim Calloway deliberately chose his time to get rid of those obnoxious fish traps that Keefe had placed at Cabbage Point. He needed a strong ebb to carry them off when their anchor cables were cut, and that particular night seemed to offer just about what he was looking for. He was even glad when the rain began. It meant that the traps would be a good distance off before Keefe could do anything about it.

There were five men at Gallway to do the job — Olaf, Jack Queens, the half-breed, George Yukat, and a young Scandinavian named Jonsrud. They had stayed in the Gallway office, keeping warm by the heating stove, watching the rain and fog over the inlet. Twilight settled early.

"Ready?" asked Tim.

The others were glad to get started.

"Better take these," he said, tossing rifles to George Yukat and Jonsrud.

All of them except Big Olaf carried guns when they left Gallway in two skiffs. Olaf had never carried a gun — he had his axe.

"Aye do plenty guede work with this axe if Aye see damn' Blue Star man," he told them.

It was a mile to Cabbage Point. An old watchman's shack stood on a spit of land, just above the reach of the spring tides. The shack had been covered by tar

202

paper once, but the tar paper had blown away, leaving cracks as thick as a man's finger through which the wind whistled, carrying its fine spray of rain. The men sat there, huddled in slickers, holding cable cutters and rifles.

Once in a while, as darkness settled, the traps with their watchman's shanties perched above became visible through the haze.

"Damn funny," muttered George Yukat, twisting a brown-paper cigarette in the shelter of his opened slicker. "I thought I saw somebody move in one of those shanty windows."

Olaf snorted: "Aye tank you bane gettin' yumpy."

Night, and there was a long wait in the darkness. At last Tim glanced at the luminous dial of his watch and stood up.

"Well, this is it."

They split into two crews — Tim and Olaf in one boat, and Queens, Jonsrud, and Yukat in the other.

Jack Queens waved with his cable cutters as they slid away through the high tide that was lapping the salt-crusted marsh grass. Judge Hartman had promised to issue an order to Keefe telling him to remove his traps from Cabbage Point, but that afternoon he admitted to Eva that it had not been done.

"But you promised me . . ."

"My dear, there are many ramifications to a thing like this that a woman would not understand. Legal aspects . . ."

"You saw Brynne Keefe? Did you tell him that Tim Calloway planned to cut those traps loose tonight?"

"Ah . . . a word, perhaps. I said something . . ."

She gave him one furious glance and ran from the room. He followed to the hall, but Eva was already disappearing up the stairs to her room. She came out a few minutes later in sou'wester and slicker, the side pocket of the slicker sagging beneath the weight of a .32-caliber revolver.

"Eva, come back here!"

But she went without a glance. He followed across the front steps and stood bareheaded as she took the shortest possible course to the Alaska Blue Star boathouse.

Tallant Keefe's launch was in its stall. She let herself down to its cockpit, and stepped on the starter. It started without hesitation. She cast off the bowline, backed into the open waters of the inlet, wheeled, and was gone into the twilight of late afternoon. A man was shouting at her from the edge of the dock, but she did not look around.

She had covered about half the distance to the Gallway when the motor commenced to backfire. The boat stopped and commenced drifting with the waves. She looked in the gas tank. It was empty.

Fog and rain hung low to the water, turning the inlet into a gray void. She could not see the shore, but she knew well enough where the wind would drift her. It would take her across to the rocky headlands east of the abandoned California-Pacific cannery, and from there it would be a four- or five-hour walk to Ketchanka, and there'd be no chance of warning Tim that his secret was out.

She had been there about a quarter hour, although it seemed longer, when her ears picked up the complaining sound of oars in oarlocks, and a boat came out of the mist. A man in slicker and Scotch cap was rowing in long, powerful sweeps. She cupped her hands and shouted a couple of times before he turned around.

When he came close, she recognized him as Big Chris, one of the laborers on the Blue Star fishing fleet.

"Yah?" he asked, peering at her through the rain. "You want coom to town?"

"I want you to row me over to Gallway."

"Ho! Aye ain't goin' to row you to no Gallway. Aye bane goin' to town for medicine. You leave anchor down on that boat and yump in. She won't get wreck with anchor draggin' maybe."

Big Chris reached over the gunwale of the launch to steady her as she stepped across. She sat facing him, and he pushed away, dipping the oars. Suddenly he paused, the oars clear of the water. He was staring into the muzzle of Eva's small-caliber revolver.

"To Gallway," she said.

Chris gulped. "Yah. Aye take you to Gallway. Aye take you damn' quick."

He wheeled around and rowed steadily into the wind, his eyes seldom leaving the revolver that glistened black and deadly in her hand.

Darkness settled in so she could scarcely see the stern of the boat. Chris rowed with dull monotony. The sea was a black, rainy wilderness. They seemed to be standing still, merely keeping even with the treadmill of the waves.

She broke the silence unexpectedly: "What are you doing out here?"

"Aye bane . . ." Chris stopped trying to figure out a lie.

"You were at the Cabbage Point traps!"

She seemed to know. "Yah."

"Was Brynne Keefe there?"

"No."

"Who was there?"

When Chris did not answer, she pointed the revolver in a more positive manner. "Who was there?"

"The Horse, he bane there. An' Spangler, an' Freeland, an' maybe four more."

"What are they planning to do?"

Big Chris was doing some thinking. He was being taken to Gallway where it might prove unhealthy for him if they discovered his part in the business, so he said: "They ban goin' do plenty shootin' when Calloway try to cut trap loose. But Aye say no! By yumpin yiminy they don' get Chris to shoot nobody. So Aye bane yump in boat an' start for town."

It sounded reasonable.

By accident or design Chris overshot Gallway, and it took him another half hour to find his way along the crooked coastline to the cannery float. A light was burning up in the cannery office.

"Come along!" she said, gesturing with her revolver.

They went inside. The building was dark and cold with the sheet metal clattering on the roof and echoing through the long length of it. They climbed a set of stairs and went inside an office heated by a little horizontal stove.

The watchman, an old gill netter named Sack, was the only one there.

"Where's Tim Calloway?"

Sack blinked at the pistol. "You won't get nothin' out of me with that weapon, young lady. I . . ."

"Hurry! Have they started over to Cabbage Point? We'll have to stop them. Keefe has a deathtrap set for them over there."

Sack cursed a little. "I told that young fool not to advertise what he was about. 'Strike at midnight,' says I, 'and let the salvage drift where she may.' I told him . . ." Sack went muttering around, maneuvering his rheumatic old shoulders into oilskins. He grabbed up an old brass anchor light and lit its wicks. "All righ', get a move on! We may be in time to stop 'em, but I doubt it."

Sack paused, looking suspiciously at Chris. "What the hell are you doing here, come to think of it?"

"Aye bane on your side now!"

The wind was in their favor, and it didn't take Chris long to row the distance to Cabbage Point. The sand spit with its stunted spruce seedlings came up as a shadow over the starboard bow, and a moment later they sighted the outline of the watchman's shanty.

Eva stood in the rocking craft to shout — but the shout did not leave her lips. Through the hiss of wind and waves burst the intense chatter of rifle fire.

CHAPTER
FIVE

Tim Calloway left the sand spit, pointing his rowboat north of the first trap so the drift of the wind would carry them to its approximate location. After a few seconds he lost sight of the other boat carrying Queens, Jonstrud, and Yukat. For a minute or two the water was a close, grayish blur, and the only thing visible was Olaf and his "guede axe", sitting hunched in the stern.

Something loomed up ahead, making him rest his oars. The boat slid on, with waves slap-slapping her sides, and thumped against the lead of the trap — that long, arm-line portion of the trap that was designed to halt the salmon on their way up the inlet, that was in fact a portion of the Ketchanka River, and drive them to the confinement of the trap's inner hearts over which the watchman's shanty was built.

Tim maneuvered the boat and followed the lead with its underwater system of pipes and nets until he found the anchor cable, now pulled tightly downstream from the force of the tide that was starting to ebb.

He went to work with the cable cutters as Olaf kept the boat steady. After a couple minutes' work the last of the steel strands parted, and the lead swung away, emitting a series of wooden groans.

208

"Now two more," said Olaf.

They followed back along the sagging lead to the square system of timbers composing the main body of the trap. They were sheltered a little here by a superstructure of bolted beams surmounted at a height of four or five feet by the dinky shanty.

The second cable was fastened to a joint in the timbers by means of an eye bolt. Tim was feeling beneath the wash of the waves trying to locate it, when Olaf thrust him out of the way, seized an axe, and chopped the bolt free with four mighty swings.

Tim crouched to balance the craft, and, as he did so, he noticed a boat over there, half submerged in the pot.

He lifted his head, and at the same instant caught a view of the window slowly being opened in the shanty up above. He seized an oar and sent the boat away. The unexpectedness of the movement knocked Olaf to the bottom of the boat. A gun whanged out from the shanty window, cutting the night with a yellow powder trail. Then more guns — a sudden, intense rattle of them, how many Tim could not tell.

The sharp movement of the boat, coupled with waves, rain, and darkness saved them from that first barrage. The men up there had delayed their ambush a trifle too long. They had expected a set-up shot during the three or four minutes that would have been required to do the job with cable cutters.

With two of the anchor cables gone, the trap swung away with the ebb. Spangler was cursing his men. Over his curses came the crash of rifles, furious but blind.

A bullet ripped through the boat below waterline, tearing out a six-inch strip of planking through which water geysered. Olaf pounced on it, stuffing his slicker into the hole. Tim Calloway heaved on the oars. A second bullet connected, making the craft shudder.

A battery electric light flashed on and swung down to focus them in its beam. The fog had blown away enough to make them a perfect target at the distance of forty yards.

Tim rested the oars, grabbed his Winchester from the six inches of water that had now rushed through the rent bottom, swung up, and fired with one, swift movement. He had been a fine shot when a boy, and his eye was not gone in the split-second press of this emergency. The light winked out with an echoing tinkle of glass. He kept on shooting, pumping the lever of the gun as fast as he could swing his right hand. The shanty was silhouetted against that lighter something that was the sky. The high velocity slugs were tearing it to splinters.

The hammer fell with an empty *click*. He had more cartridges in his Mackinaw pocket. He dug under his slicker for them and stuffed them in the magazine with slippery cold fingers.

In a second's lull he picked up the sound of shooting over by the number two trap. So they had been in wait at both of them!

"Ol' boat, she's bane swamp," moaned Olaf.

It was taking water rapidly through its splintered planking. It commenced listing slowly to one side, the waves lapping over the gunwale.

210

No more shooting now up in the shanty. The trap was still swinging away. For a moment the fog and darkness covered it. Tim and Olaf sat still, not daring to row for fear of swamping the boat. They drifted, the trap came again in sight, hanging on its one cable. They were carried toward it.

Another light flashed on — probably the watchman's light moved from the other side of the shanty. It swept the water, swinging in slow arcs, reaching farther and farther out. Whoever operated that light evidently did not suspect the helpless nature of the boat. Certainly he had no idea it was being carried in right beneath his nose.

"Here we come!" muttered Tim, sitting very still.

The boat came to rest against the pot timbers as the electric beam swept like a streak of milk through the mist and rain overhead. Tim and Olaf climbed out, leaving their cable cutters behind. They were lucky to escape with weapons and their lives.

A corner of the shack was towards them not more than twelve or fifteen feet away. Their nearness and the brightness of the battery light kept them from being seen. Spangler was still cursing his men. His hard, gunman's face was dimly revealed in the open window by the fog reflections of the light beam.

"Aye bet that damn' girl tip off Blue Star . . . ," started Olaf.

"Choke it off," whispered Tim.

He had the same thought. In some manner Keefe had found out that this would be the night. Tim had told the girl he would cut them loose on the week's best

211

ebb unless her uncle ordered Keefe to remove them. He knew now that he was a fool for having trusted her. Her whole play — her professed love for him, the irate Tallant had been a frame-up.

"We're in a hell of a fix now," he said under his breath, walking the slippery, floating timbers.

Then he remembered about that other rowboat. It was over beside the framework that held up the shack. He walked that way, balancing.

"Har," muttered Olaf, trying to hold him back from what he considered certain death from the shanty.

"The boat," he whispered to Olaf.

The tide was running more swiftly now. They could feel the tug of it, snapping against the shore cable.

A voice from above: "I tell you, this trap is moving! We'll be in a hell of a shape if it breaks free in an ebb like this."

"Where are your guts?" snarled Spangler.

"Guts be damned. I'd rather be a live coward than a stiff hero floating out Cape March with this heap of kindling around me."

Tim made it to the shanty and stooped to pass beneath. A platform of rough boards had been built there. Radiating from it were planks leading to the tunnel, the heart, and the spiller of the trap.

He waited until he felt the press of Olaf against him, then he went on, pulling the boat in by its tie rope. He bailed with a bucket that had been left in the boat for that purpose, and Olaf lent a hand, dipping with his sou'wester. The regular *splash-splash* of dipped water was lost in the general slap of waves.

212

He noticed Olaf staring upstream. There was something up there. A mass of timbers coming. It was that number two trap. Queens had succeeded in cutting it free.

The electric beam came to rest on it, and there followed a wild cursing up above.

"It's the other trap! Let's get out of here! Why, it'll crack that lone cable of ours like nothing!"

"Hurry, Olaf," Tim muttered.

"Yah."

Olaf clapped his sou'wester back on his head. No more time to bail — they were clomping to get out up above.

The boat was still a third full of water. It would have been hard to lift with good footing; here it was just a rotten gamble. But there was nothing else for it. A set of legs were thrust down from the trap door.

"Ready?" asked Tim.

"Yah."

They lifted. The boat balanced for a ragged instant, and started to slide back.

"Heave!" shouted Tim.

Olaf roared, and with a mighty swing of his shoulders lifted it over the timber. Tim slid it on down and it hit the open water.

He had an impression of a man dropping to the platform behind him. Spangler. The gunman reached inside his slicker for the butt of a revolver as Tim and Olaf jumped into the boat. Spangler came up with his gun. Tim's Winchester was back on the platform. His revolver was in his slicker pocket, and there was no getting it in time. Spangler's range was point-blank, so Tim simply went shoulder first into the bottom of the boat with its six inches of water.

To Tim, in the bottom of the boat, the explosion seemed far away. He came to his knees, trying to tear the revolver from his pocket. Olaf was piled on top of him, and that made it all the tougher.

He could see Spangler getting set to center the next one. Olaf sprang up, poising his axe. He flung it as a lesser man might fling a knife. Its head made a momentary, steely flash in the gloom, and it struck, snapping Spangler so he doubled over.

Olaf emitted a roar and crouched as though he intended to plunge back onto the platform. Tim slammed him down. He shoved free and heaved on the oars that had been hanging in the locks.

The hulk of number two trap, riding silently in the water, was almost upon them. Spangler came to one elbow, shooting until his gun was empty. The rapid explosions cast a repeated glow lighting his pain-twisted features.

Tim had no time to worry about bullets. It was a close battle trying to escape the long lead and nettings of the drifting trap. With a final heave at his oars he made open water. Then he rested, breathing a prayer of thanksgiving.

All shooting had stopped. Voices were shouting. A few seconds were filled with the groan of colliding timbers. He wondered if that one cable would hold the weight of both traps, after all. There came a deep *boom* like a single blow struck to a bass drum. That was the cable, snapping far beneath the water.

"Hell of a spot, even for fellows like that," Tim muttered. "I wish I could take them off."

"Aye tank ol' devil take care his own," said Olaf. "They won't drown, but Aye bet they get pretty damn' chilly by morning."

Tim cupped his hands and shouted Jack Queens's name. Distantly, through wind and rain, came the answer. He kept shouting and getting answers all the way back to the sand spit. Jack was there with all his men, and three others besides.

"They didn't show too much fight after I got two of those cables cut." Jack grinned.

Back at the Gallway cannery float a third boat came in sight. Tim looked with amazement as Eva Hartman came ashore. A sudden anger swept him. She had given the tipoff to Keefe, and now she was there to watch the outcome — and in a skiff rowed by Big Chris, the Blue Star fink.

"Oh, Tim!" she cried, starting towards him, her long, black slicker flapping around her legs.

There was something in his eyes that made her stop.

He said: "Yes, I'm here. Safe. And those traps of your future father-in-law's are on their way to the sea. Go back and tell him that some of his best killers are trapped on them. Maybe he'd like to go out to Cape March tomorrow morning and pick them up."

"Tim! You don't think . . . ?"

"I think you're a Keefe spy!"

She flared with defensive anger. It was all so plain to her — it seemed that it should be plain to him, too. She decided that she hated him. She tried to find words that would tell how she felt, but she stood there, mute, and watched while he led his sodden crowd toward the cannery building.

Big Chris came and tapped her on the elbow. "Aye tank he don' mean all that. Aye skal tell him plenty. You coom on inside, an' . . ."

"I wouldn't go in there if . . . here, you row me back to Ketchanka!"

"Aye tank you better . . ."

"Row me back to Ketchanka!"

Chris shrugged heavily. "OK. Aye skal do." He climbed back in the rowboat and rocked on the oars. "Damn. Aye don' ban get that drink very fas'."

CHAPTER
SIX

Spring arrived with a warm breath from the Pacific. With it came the cannery supply ships to heap docks with goods and boom Fish Alley with white man and Oriental, flush with their advance pay. Gallway, which had been forlorn and abandoned, was suddenly a rush of activity. Hers was a historic name in the cannery business, and there was no trouble in finding merchants who would gamble on the year's salmon run.

On the second supply ship, Jack Queens came up from Seattle where he had lined up a Chinese labor contract and made a deal of the season's pack. He asked about Keefe, and learned that the master of the Blue Star had caused no trouble. Keefe had recently expanded, purchasing canneries at Stikine and Istikut, and he apparently had little time to worry about Gallway.

It was only a breather, though. They knew that. Ketchanka meant more to Keefe than all else combined.

"They tell me in Seattle that Keefe contracted to pack two hundred and fifty thousand cases," Queens said.

"That much? Why, that's an average season for Blue Star and Gallway combined!"

"Sure. He wasn't figuring on Gallway being open. You know what it means, don't you?"

Tim knew what it meant. It meant that Keefe would have to get the entire catch or lose his pants.

Queens shook his head. "We have a fight on our hands, Tim. He'll try to block us off. He'll try to shoot us off. He'll pirate our traps."

Tim grinned, rubbing his strong young hands. "And maybe we'll do a little fightin on our own."

Next morning they watched with binoculars as a couple of Keefe tugs towed a salmon trap to the foot of Marluk Island over to the southwest of Gallway.

"I can't figure that out," said Tim. "That Marluk run has always been spotty."

That was true. When the great run of salmon came up the Ketchanka to their spawning ground, their habit was to follow the north shore along Cabbage Point, and leave Marluk pretty much alone.

"He's no fool," Jack Queens said. "If he builds at Marluk, he must know where the fish are coming from."

Then one day there was a surge of life from the deep Pacific, and the mystery of the Marluk traps was forgotten. The yearly salmon run had commenced.

The run was poor and spotty along the coast. The big, pile-driven traps that Tim had repaired and placed in operation on Cape March and Blair Island took only a scattering of fish. The floating traps of Blue Star, and its Olson subsidiary were also ignored, but the

218

Calloway tender was kept busy bailing from the traps at Cabbage Point. Fish from those traps inundated the plant, and some of the overflow were taken to Queens's little cannery over by the Mission.

"I never saw anything like it," Queens said after it had continued like that for two weeks. "They're skunked all along the coast. Everybody. Not a standing trap worth the lifting. Why, they're catching more cod and dogfish than salmon. Blue Star is operating at a third of capacity." He shook his head. "Luck's a funny thing. It was against your dad for six solid years. Now it looks like it was the Calloway turn at last."

However, if Jack Queens had known of a conference then taking place in Brynne Keefe's office, his exuberance would have turned to alarm. There were five of them at that conference, and one of them was Tallant Keefe. When it was finished, he dropped around to one of his favorite honky-tonks on Fish Alley for a bit of excitement, and then went bravely forward to call on Eva Hartman.

"The pater is a tough one for competition." He chuckled expansively. "Even the time-honored whims of the running salmon can't phase him. You know how they've been filling those Gallway traps on the north shore without giving Blue Star as much as a flip of their fins? Well, Pater is going to change all that."

"I'm afraid even your father would have a hard time changing the whims of a salmon run."

"But that's where you're wrong, old girl. For do you know what he plans? Now, not a word about it, mind you. It's supposed to be a bit of a surprise for that young fellow over at Gallway. He's going to stretch webbing all the way from the north shore to Marluk Island."

"But it's against the law to block off a river."

"Pater, my dear, makes his own laws. However, we're not blocking the river. That is merely half the channel, and on tidewater at that. The salmon still have the privilege of following the south shore, or, if they prefer, they can swim inside those traps we thoughfully towed to Marluk."

Tallant lolled back in a spring-filled chair, lighted a cigarette, and blew smoke lazily toward the ceiling. "Oh, that pater of mine is the tough operator, though I won't pretend I didn't have a part in this little scheme myself." He looked at Eva through a gray haze of cigarette smoke. "Come, girl! You don't seem half as happy as I thought you would. You want us to beat that pup, don't you?"

"Yes, but . . ."

"But what?"

"I wanted you to do it fairly!"

Tallant laughed tolerantly, reaching for her hand to pull her towards him. "Oh come, now. This is the salmon business. You've heard that old saying . . . 'There is no law of God nor man north of Fifty-Three!'"

Eva had been trying to tell herself that she hated Tim Calloway, and that she really did care very much for Tallant Keefe, but she was relieved when he finally decided to leave. Her uncle was still at work in his office, so she knocked and went in.

"What is the law that pertains to blocking a channel with a net?" she asked him.

"Why, you know as well as I do. If a river channel is blocked, the salmon will be prevented from running to their spawning grounds. In a few years there would be no salmon at all."

"Did you know that Keefe was planning to block the channel from the north bank all the way to Marluk Island?"

"Nonsense! It is utterly infeasible. If Tallant told you that, he was merely stringing you along. No, my girl, you toddle up to bed and think no more about it."

But infeasible or not, two days later when Eva took a run over to Blue Star village, she saw the cannery working to speed with tons of gleaming, silvery salmon on the sorting floor, while busy tenders kept shuttling fish over from the Marluk traps.

Tallant Keefe was sitting with his back against a piling, a handsome figure in his sports clothes.

"Oh, I say!" He grinned. "Business here is picking up, although I hear that Gallway isn't catching enough fish in a day to stink a Chinaman's hands."

It was evening when she got back to the Government House. Her uncle's office door was partly open, so she went in without knocking. A familiar voice brought her up qucikly. She looked up at Tim Calloway.

She quickly turned and left the room.

"Wait!" He was following her with long strides.

She tried to get up the stairs, but he blocked the way. There was something about his honest, snub-nosed smile that made it hard to stay angry with him.

He said: "Big Chris told me about picking you up in his boat. He said you were on your way to warn us. I'd have realized, if I hadn't been so Irish dumb. I'm awfully sorry for the things I said that night."

"Will you get out of my way?"

"No. And Eva, listen . . ."

She ducked around him and started up the stairs. She kept telling herself that she was angry, but there was something clean and strong about the man that called strongly to her. She turned for a parting shot.

"In other words, you would believe Big Chris but not me?"

"Listen, Eva! That's all wrong. I . . ."

Judge Hartman grabbed him by the elbow.

"You came here on business, didn't you? If that business is completed, I'll thank you to leave my house."

"*Our* house!" Tim reminded him. "I'm a citizen, too, you know."

Eva stopped after she was out of sight beyond the top of the stairs. Somehow she was hoping Tim would follow her, although she knew he wouldn't. She listened to the front door close several moments later, and the thump of his boots across the porch. She went to the window of the spare room from which she could see the series of stone steps leading down to the upper end of Fish Alley.

It was summer, and the night had no real darkness. She watched Tim walk swiftly, with a sinuous, animal grace. He seemed to know where he was going.

222

She sat in her room for a while, then she went back down the stairs and asked: "What did he want?"

"Oh, the same foolishness about a net being stretched from the north shore to Marluk Island."

"What action are you going to take?"

Hartman cleared his throat. "Why I intend to check up with Mister Keefe to see whether there's any truth to the story."

"Did Mister Calloway say what he planned to do?"

"Pah! He performed his usual chest-thumping. The braggart! Said he'd go up there with the crew and cut the net free from the north shore if it isn't gone by midnight tonight. Midnight! Why, that's only a couple of hours."

Eva knew by some things that Tallant had said that Brynne Keefe was taking no chances this time. He had placed Spangler and a gang of gunmen at the anchor spots to take care of developments. There was no use arguing with her uncle. He was not a dishonest man, but it was hard for one, lone U.S. commissioner to stand up against power like Keefe wielded. She didn't stop to reason what she was going to do. She said good night to him, and left quietly by the front door.

Once at the stone steps leading down to Fish Alley, she commenced to run. Cannery workers — that flotsam of the North — hooted at her. She ran past shacks with big front windows where women sat with lights behind them, past gambling dens, and saloons, and Chinese cafés. There were a dozen men in sight on the public docks, but none of them was Tim Calloway. His boat was not tied up at the float. She listened. In the distance the *putt-putt* of an outboard motor was dying away.

"Was that Tim Calloway who just left?" she asked a Japanese stevedore.

"Yes. That Calloway."

She had intended to warn him of the danger that awaited at that northern net anchor. It was too late now. She consoled herself by thinking that Tim was the kind who could take care of himself.

CHAPTER
SEVEN

Tim swung his outboard to the cannery float at Gallway and strode across the docks where a good two-thirds of the crew was lying around with nothing to do. Beneath a gasoline floodlight an enterprising Chinese had started a fan-tan game. From inside came the *clank* of cannery machinery as one line kept going on salmon that trickled in from the standing traps along the coast.

He found Jack Queens moodily contemplating the scene from a catwalk that ran along the front of the building.

"What did His Honor have to say?" he asked.

"Just what we expected."

Queens shrugged. "Well, we entered our complaint, and that's the important thing, if this business ever ends up in court . . . which I doubt."

"Did you locate the north anchor of the webbing?"

"Sure. But it's no good, Tim. That damned Keefe has ten men down there, and what I mean they're heeled."

Tim scratched his head thoughtfully. "How well do you love that seiner boat of yours?"

225

"It's as much yours as mine. If we lose it, we'll be half out of business."

"And if that net stays, we'll be *all* out of business."

"The boat hasn't power enough to drag the net free, if that's what you have in mind. It's held by a dead-weighted three-inch hawser, and . . ."

"Never mind that. Just send one of the boys in for all the dynamite we have, and come down here with me."

The seiner was one of the standard fifty-footers of the Alaskan coast. She had a prow fitted with a kelp knife to cut her way through weeds. She stunk of fish, needed a coat of paint, but her big workhouse motor purred like a butcher shop cat.

"What the hell are you going to do with all that powder?" Queens asked when he saw a Filipino trucking out two 100-pound cases.

"I'm going to hook it on the anchor with a long fuse. That kelp knife on the prow should cut our way through the top of the net, and I dare say that two hundred pounds of nitro hooked to the bottom should do the business to that three-inch hawser."

In an hour they were ready. The cases of dynamite were roped near the top of the anchor. Extending from the top case was three feet of double underwater fuse. A Danish fish grader who had once been powder-monkey in the gold mines of Juneau sat with his back against the cases, an unlighted fuse spitter extending from the pocket of his shirt. Down below the engineer was adjusting the carburetors a little and revving up the motor.

"Let it go!" called Tim.

They set out as though it were one of the regular trips across to the main channel, and thence either to Cape March or the Mission. A faint, saffron glow hung on the midnight horizon but the water was purplish with darkness.

Scarcely a word was spoken aboard the seiner. It slowly increased its speed until the propeller was boiling under full throttle.

"That anchor will pull us apart like a string of sausages when she hits bottom," muttered Queens.

Tim laughed. He felt pretty good about it all now that they were started.

"The nitro has enough buoyancy to balance it. She'll sink as gently as a dandelion seed."

Off to the left was the foot of Marluk Island and the new traps with which Keefe was hogging the deflected salmon run. To the right was the mainland with a little, silvery line of froth showing where water and shore met.

The helmsman swung sharply at the foot of the island, and raced up the right-hand channel. Tim watched for the net, knowing its approximate location even though it was too dark to see its line of floats.

Someone was shouting over on the bank. The Dane had lighted his spitter fuse. He crouched there, eyes on Tim.

Tim gave him a hand signal. The Dane bent and quickly applied the spitter to the notched fuses. He crouched back as they hissed with a reddish flame that crept with menacing speed toward the big, wooden boxes.

There was a yellow flash of light from on shore, a clank and whine of a high-powered bullet striking steel and glancing away. A second later came the *ka-whang* of a rifle.

"We'll be blown to Ketchanka if a bullet hits this powder!" The Dane grinned.

Other guns then, a sudden fury of them, too many to count. They tore splinters, whanged steel plates, and glanced away, whining like yellow jackets. Tim bent over the explosive, the Dane beside him. From a boiler room port someone was returning the fire with unknown results.

A string of grayish streaks came in sight over the bow. Those were the net floats. Tim said something. The Dane took one side, and himself the other. Anchor, powder, and hissing fuse were tossed over the stern. It lit with a splash and bobbed a couple of times in the boiling wake, a coil of medium rope unwinding after it. The rope came tight and twanged like a banjo string. Then it relaxed a trifle, showing that anchor and explosive were skimming the bottom.

There was a momentary hesitation and the boat veered a few degrees as the kelp knives sliced through the top four feet of webbing. The anchor rope whipped, grew tight, and snapped.

They were going away now. The rifles kept popping away, but the range made them ineffectual. Finally the shooting stopped, and there was no sound except the full throttle hum of motors and the swish of wake.

Everyone except Tim and the Dane had taken cover, praying that no bullet would strike the dynamite. They crawled from the hatch now, watching the water astern.

It seemed like a long time. The Dane crouched on his knees, lips moving as he counted. He lifted one hand and held it poised. With an exclamation, he dropped it.

There were a few seconds of waiting. Then, with a deep rumble, the placid waters of the inlet erupted in a tall geyser of froth.

"*Yo-ho!*" shouted the Dane. "That call for one drink whiskey for eberybody, hey?"

Queens did a jig step and answered: "A drink be damned. Take us over to town and I'll make it an imperial quart."

Judge Hartman had tried to find Brynne Keefe that night, but Keefe was at Istikut where his new cannery was suffering from fish famine. So the judge decided to play a few hands of solo at the Silver Salmon.

It was there that he heard the distant roar of dynamite and, an hour or so later, received news of the destruction of the net.

"Well?" asked Fred Mayfair, operator of a saltery up the coast, lifting his eyebrows at the judge. "What do you do in a case like that?"

Hartman did not answer. What, indeed, should a commissioner do about a man who unlawfully dynamited an unlawful net?

Mayfair thereupon went on to say something that caused Judge Hartman's spine to become as rigid as a pike-pole.

"In a month's time the run will be over. If this month goes like the last one, Keefe will be flat broke while Tim Calloway and Jack Queens will be the top dogs in Ketchanka. That's the salmon business for you!"

As a judge down in the States, Hartman had served in awe of the great corporations. "They're the backbone of our stable economy!" he had been fond of saying in his philosophical moments. When he was sent north on this political job, it was natural for him to sympathize with Keefe. Now, if Keefe went under . . .

Next morning at breakfast he said: "Eva, don't you think you're being too stern with that Tim Calloway? After all, he has great possibilities, that lad. A fine, upstanding young man, Eva!"

Eva almost dropped her coffee cup in amazement.

Jack Queens walked across the Gallway float four days later and asked Tim Calloway if he'd ever heard of a man making twenty consecutive passes at roulette.

"No. Why?"

"Because that's just what we're doing in the fish business. I was out looking at that Cape Shelton standing trap of ours. It's running full, while that Blue Star trap license five fifty-three, a few miles down the coast, isn't getting a smell."

"They're doing better than we are at Cape March."

"Oh, what the hell? They have to pack twice as many fish in order to make their contract, don't they?"

About noon the tender ran over to Shelton, but it came back empty reporting that a pirate craft had raided the trap, and lifted every fin.

"He put up a fight, that watchman," said the skipper, "but what could you expect? They opened up on him with a dozen rifles. You should see that shanty of his. Riddled like grandma's colander. What a mess."

"What did the pirate craft look like?" Tim asked.

"Couldn't tell. She was a fifty-footer, but her pilot house was covered with tarps, and they had gunny sacks hung over her lettering."

Salmon pirates had always operated along the Alaskan coast, and it was not unusual to have a couple of traps lifted in a season. Tim thought little more about the matter until next day when the two standing traps on Cape March were raided, as was a floater up the river.

To check up, he ran his outboard along the shore to Blue Star village. No fish famine there. No loafers along the float, and the iron chinks were clinking along in fine style.

At Cabbage Point the traps were still taking good numbers of salmon, so Gallway kept going on a restricted basis.

Tim tried to find extra men to serve guard duty on coastal traps, but none wanted the job. Word had gone around that King Salmon Keefe was on the kill, and who would risk his life for Gallway salmon even at triple wages? At the end of a day's search, Tim returned with three men he had hired at $30 a day.

"By golly, Aye tank we go broke at that rate," moaned Olaf.

"We have to get up the pack!" Tim answered with short temper.

He armed the men and sent them to the most valuable trap along the coast — the one at the head of Blair Island.

Next day the masked seiner lifted the two traps at Cape March, and at midnight a powerboat made a try at the number two at Cabbage Point, but it was finally driven off by rifle fire from the shore.

The salmon war was the only topic of conversation in Ketchanka. Keefe was fighting off his streak of luck. He was pirating every fish he could locate, trying to keep his over-expanded empire from collapsing. At every street corner Eva heard men talking salmon war, she heard it in every parlor on Nob Hill, and Tallant was exultant with the approaching Blue Star victory when he came each evening to call.

"Is Blue Star pirating those Gallway traps?" she asked him one night. She was determined to get to the bottom.

"Blue Star? Oh come, girl! You can't accuse us of anything like that. There have always been pirates along the Alaska coast."

"I notice none of your traps have been lifted."

"But we haven't been getting the run."

"Then why are your canneries running full for the first time this season?"

"Well, I'll tell you, Eva. We buy fish from independents when they become available. If somebody wheels up with a hold filled with fish, we don't look into their pedigrees before signing a check."

As soon as Tallant left, the Chinese houseboy padded in and motioned Eva to the kitchen. There, by the rear

232

door, sat Big Chris, his face so bruised she had to look twice to recognize him.

"Chris!"

"Aye bane have fight," he said, trying not to move his jaw too much. "Those Holgar The Horse beat me up plenty."

"Why did you come here? If you want to see the judge . . ."

"Aye don' want see no judge. Aye yust want get even wit' those damn' Blue Star pirate. So Aye coom see you. Maybe you tell somebody else."

He didn't mention Tim's name, but it was obvious that Tim was who he meant.

"Tell what?"

" 'Bout goin' to raid big Blair Island standin' trap. Holgar The Horse, he coom to me an' say . . . 'Chris, tomorrow we skal raid Blair Island.' Aye bane tell him Calloway have four, five guard on that trap with rifle. He say . . . 'We got eight, ten men with rifle and plenty dynamite, you bet. We goin' have big boss on boat, too.' But Aye say . . . 'No. Aye don' skal work for Blue Star now. Aye skal goin' get yob on halibut trooler and to hell with ol' rough stuff. Aye yust goin' to be honest fisherman from har out.' Then next ting Holgar bane hit me. Yumpin yiminy, Aye don't know what happen from then on, but I guess it bane one hell of a fight."

"So to get even you came to tell me. Why didn't you go to Gallway?"

"Maybe they don' believe me. Maybe Calloway say . . . 'That damn Chris, he's Blue Star pirate.' "

Eva walked to the hall door and called: "Uncle!"

"Aye don' want no more trouble, by golly. Aye yust want yob on halibut trooler . . ."

"Sit down!"

Chris obeyed, easing himself to the edge of a kitchen chair, his purpled eyes apprehensively on the door as Judge Hartman approached.

"Tell him about it," Eva commanded.

"No! It bane yust like tellin' story to ol' King Salmon Keefe."

The judge made a gesture showing how this remark irritated him. "Nonsense. You can be perfectly frank with me. Your words will never be carried beyond this room."

Chris went ahead and told his story, eyeing the judge apprehensively, twisting his hat as though he were trying to wring water out of it.

"Well?" asked Eva when he was through and the judge had spent some time pondering.

The judge stood straight with fine resolve. "Why, I intend to look into this."

"To go to Keefe?"

"No! I will take the government launch out there along the coast where I can watch that trap through binoculars. I intend to see exactly what goes on, and, when I get the facts, I will make a full and complete report to the United States government."

Actually the judge's resolve was not as high as he made it sound. He intended to get the facts — and then wait. If Keefe won out, he would do nothing. If, however, it looked as though Blue Star was going on the rocks, he could raise himself in Tim Calloway's good graces by getting in on the kill.

The judge was pleased with himself for having thought of this fine means of hedging. He chuckled to himself as he put on warm clothing, for even in midsummer the breezes were chilly on that northern sea. He went downstairs with his long, ten-power binoculars tossed over his shoulder, and Eva and Chris were waiting for him.

There was a slight mist hanging to the surface as they set out through the near darkness in the government launch. They rounded Cape March and found a hiding place in a little-used channel between the mainland and the rocky shore of Blair Island.

About a half mile away was the extensive framework of the Calloway standing trap. Like most coastal traps, it was constructed of pile-driven spruce poles that extended twenty or twenty-five feet upward from the surface of the water. Atop the poles were wandering platforms of log and plank. Grayish netting hung in apparent disorder. Smoke commenced coming from the tar paper covered watchman's shanty atop the trap indicating that breakfast was being prepared.

"What do they eat?" asked Eva with natural woman's interest.

"Plenty geude, fresh salmon fish, you bet." Chris grinned.

After a few minutes the judge handed the binoculars to Eva and pointed across the water. Even without the binoculars she could make out something coming toward them from the direction of Cape March.

Four men came from the trap shanty and stood watching. They didn't seem to be alarmed. The boat approached, and tied up at the spiller.

"Aye tank it bane yust ol' Gallway boat," said Chris.

The boat drained the catch aboard. Someone climbed the trap ladder to sign for the fish, and the boat pulled away.

"Well, is that an example of your piracy?" the judge snorted.

"You tank you go now?"

"Wait!" commanded Eva.

In scarcely a quarter hour a second boat came in sight and headed toward the trap — it was a grayish seiner with part of its superstructures masked by tarps.

Chris chuckled to himself. "Blue Star pirate ban yust too late this time, by golly."

The boat swung close, and the *whang* of a high-speed rifle bounded across the water.

"Good heavens!" said the judge.

"That one was yust warning. They yust show trap man they ain't foolin'."

It took the skipper of the masked craft two or three minutes to ascertain there were no fish in the spiller.

Chris sat chuckling. "That bane good yoke on ol' King Salmon Keefe. He's on that boat, Aye guess."

The judge was studying the men on deck. He saw someone who made him go tense.

"Keefe?" asked Eva.

"Yes. And Tallant is there, too."

The pirate boat swung clear of the trap and nosed along close to shore. They expected it to swing to the channel west of Blair Island, but instead it came straight on, sliding through a patch of kelp, picking its way up the narrow channel almost toward the rocks where the government launch was hiding.

"Aye tank we better get out of here," said Chris, reaching to turn on the ignition.

Eva stopped him. "There's no use trying to get away. They'd run us down."

At a distance of forty or fifty yards the pilot shouted and jingled the engine bells. He had seen the low-hulled government boat there among the rocks.

Chris waited no longer. He peeled off his coat and plunged into the cold sea. He shook off the remainder of his clothes as he swam, feeling his way around submerged rocks. Half a dozen men came through the hatch of the seiner.

"It's Miss Hartman and the judge!" Freeland shouted.

Lockley was there, and The Horse, and Demart, and several others. It was a moment before Brynne Keefe appeared. He was roughly dressed in a gray sweater, laced trousers, and knee boots. Tallant came up a moment later to stand at his father's side. Then Spangler, carrying two guns instead of his usual one.

"Lower a boat!" Keefe barked.

The crew rushed to obey him. It was plain he was in no mood to trifle after his bad luck back at the trap.

Freeland and Spangler rowed the skiff over. Spangler looked at the judge and growled: "Climb aboard!"

The judge was very pale, but he summoned enough of his faltering dignity to say: "Sir! I have every intention of returning to Ketchanka by the same conveyance in which I came. And as for . . ."

Spangler muttered a vile word and flipped a gun from his shoulder holster. "You're goin' aboard the seiner, Judge, one way or another."

The judge hurried to board the skiff, and Eva followed him. It took only a minute or so to reach the seiner.

Brynne Keefe stood with feet widely apart, watching as they were boosted aboard. The expression in his eyes gave Eva a chill. It was the same inhuman expression she had seen there that night Tim Calloway had refused his handshake.

"You found out enough to satisfy your curiosity?" he asked.

The judge stammered: "I don't know what you . . ."

"Your niece has always been out to cut my throat. She had my son fooled, but she never fooled me. You understand that your action today leaves me only one course. I have often heard you comment on the value of the large corporations, Judge. Therefore, I know you will be the first to appreciate that the existence of Alaska Blue Star means more to the country than a pair of lives. You . . ."

"Dad!" Tallant had gone a trifle pale. "What are you talking about?"

"Son, go below! This is once when you're not going to interfere with my expedient methods."

238

"The judge, maybe, but Lord . . . you can't do such a thing with a woman!"

"The fact that she is a woman merely makes it more unpleasant."

CHAPTER
EIGHT

The Horse stalked over, looking at Keefe with his dull eyes. He was bruised up considerably with great purple and red blotches where Big Chris had connected.

"Aye say something, yah."

"Well?"

"Aye tank other feller tell."

"What other fellow?"

"Big Chris. He yump overboard from government boat when we stop. Maybe he go to town, tell . . ."

"Why didn't you say something before, you fool?"

"Aye don' know. Aye tank . . ."

"There he is!" shouted Freeland.

Chris had reached waist-deep water and was wading 250 yards away. Spangler ran to the gun rack beside the hatch, grabbed an .06, aimed, pressed the trigger. The bullet tore a streak of froth a few inches to Chris's right. He plunged forward, half swimming around a cluster of glistening black stones. Other men pumped bullets. Chris went on, splashing knee-deep water, fighting sticky sand until he disappeared into the evergreens growing close to the shore.

Keefe cursed. He looked around for someone on whom to vent his wrath. His eyes fell on The Horse. He set his heels, and swung a terrific right to The Horse's jaw.

The Horse reeled, backpedaling, coming down heavily on his heels so that the entire boat trembled in the water. He struck the cabin and slid down with eyes glazed like a steer's under the mallet.

"Well, where do we go from here?" asked Tallant.

Brynne Keefe gestured at Eva and the judge. "Take them below." He strode half the length of the boat, then stood looking into the fish hold. It was empty save for the accumulated slime and odors of the previous day's thefts. He then answered his son's question. "If you think I'm going back to Blue Star village without a haul, you're wrong. There isn't much left of the season. If Blue Star goes as many as three days without capacity, it fails in its salmon pack." He shook his hands under Tallant's nose. "I've won a fortune with my hands. Torn it from these cold waters despite the worst my competitors could throw at me. They call me a thief, a pirate, a killer. But I'm a businessman. It's men like me who make the backbone of this country. And I'm not going to be beaten because some punk kid prevents me from meeting a flock of paper obligations to a lot of woman-fingered bankers down in Frisco! We're going to get in a haul today." He smiled grimly, hands on hips. "And I have an idea where we're going to get it."

"Pater, may I be so bold . . . ?"

"We're going to lift those traps at Cabbage Point."

"Right in full sight of Gallway and . . ."

"Yes, and with the commissioner himself locked in our hold. Why, this is first-rate, Tallant. The judge likes to be on the winning side, and here he is!"

The sun was making a gleaming yellow path across the waters of the inlet when they turned around the eastern end of Marluk Island and headed for the floating traps at Cabbage Point. Keefe nervously paced the deck, repeatedly peering through the dissolving mists to see if any unusual precautions had been taken for the protection of the trap. There was a watchman on each of them, of course, but Gallway was more than a mile away.

The watchman had come from the shanty and was looking at them through binoculars.

"This will be easy." Tallant grinned.

"Too damned easy!" growled Keefe.

"We'd better get below. No use in advertising . . ."

"The hell with it! I'll take what I want, and I don't care who sees me."

Tallant winked to Spangler. He was proud of his father — the man who took what he wanted! Quoth Tallant: "There's never a law of God nor man north of Fifty-Three."

A gunshot rattled out somewhere in the hold. Tallant and his father both spun around.

"Who fired that shot?" barked Keefe.

The watchman in the floating trap hurried back to his cabin. Lockley ran below to investigate. He could be heard booting on a door.

"It's the judge!" shouted Lockley, heaving against the door of the chart room with his shoulder. "They've locked themselves in . . . firing from the port to warn Gallway."

"Stay away from that door!" It was Eva's voice. Something about it told Lockley she was not joking. The gun cracked, tearing splinters from the panel closest his shoulder.

"Holy bald-headed hell," muttered Freeland, peering down the hatch. "How'd you like to have her for a wife?"

Tallant laughed and whacked the leg of his sports trousers. "It's lucky for us salmon pirates that the judge isn't that tough."

Keefe laughed grimly at his son's words. He admired strength. He admired that girl down there, just as he despised the judge.

"Leave them alone, Lockley! We've had enough shooting to stir up the hornets as it is."

The floating trap was only a couple hundred yards away now. There came a *whang* from the watchman's rifle — a warning bullet across the bow.

Four of the men took places in protection of some netting bales. Others crouched in the cockpit or in the cover of the hatch. They were all schooled in jobs like this, and that one rifle didn't sound too tough.

Another fifty yards, and the four rifles opened up. The high-velocity, soft-nose bullets were tearing the shack to slivers. The watchman stayed low, and Keefe knew by experience he would cause little more trouble barring the arrival of reinforcements.

He watched Gallway. Men were running across the float. One of them was tall Tim Calloway. Someone came lugging a couple or three rifles. They were climbing aboard the snub-nosed cannery tender.

The side of the pirate craft rubbed the timbers of the spiller and it was made fast.

"Hurry with that brailer!" shouted Keefe.

Keefe stood near the edge and looked down into the transparent waters. The net-made compartment was seething with fish. It would be a great haul, and more than that, a daring haul — but they must hurry, hurry!

The first scoop of fish showered through the air, and the slimy bottom of the hold came to life with flip-flopping salmon. The brailer again. Over at Gallway the tender was just pulling from the float. Another scoop — a mighty one — but the elevating mechanism had stopped. Keefe spotted the trouble. One of the ropes had run afoul of its block.

"The block! You fools!" screamed Keefe as the operator put on more power, making the jam worse.

Nobody seemed to know what to do, so Keefe swung up, hand over hand, and heaved on the fouled rope.

"Power!" he bellowed.

The winch operator tossed his lever, and the rope promptly locked again.

The tender had left Gallway by then and had covered a third of the distance.

"To hell with it!" shouted Freeland. "Let's get out of here before . . ."

Keefe cursed and snapped the rope free. He dropped back to the deck and struck Freeland with his fist so that he backpedaled and sprawled across one of the bales of webbing up forward.

"I'm issuing the orders! We'll stay until these fish have been lifted . . . every fin of them. Tim Calloway will never see the day he chased Brynne Keefe from his own waters."

Encouraged by the prospect of help, and by the preoccupation of the men aboard the seiner, the watchman raised up from the plank bulwark at the base of the shack and sent a bullet screaming across the deck. Spangler and Demart opened up again.

"Work that brailer!" Keefe shouted, his feet spread widely, ignoring the whine of high-velocity bullets.

The tender from Gallway was in range, but she had not opened fire. She was coming full speed, her twin screws sending boiling fountains of water out behind.

Spangler turned his attention to it and aimed a bullet at her cabin. A couple of rifles aboard the tender opened up in answer. Tallant plunged down the hatch to cover. Spangler was hit by a bullet from the watchman. He staggered up, dragging his rifle, and plunged headfirst into the hold amid a seething fifteen inches of fish. In seconds he had disappeared as though in quicksand.

Now at last Keefe took to cover. He stepped around the cabin and waited there, a long-barreled .38 Magnum revolver in his hand. There was a cold smile on his lips. He was waiting for one shot. Just one.

The tender came straight on — a powerful little workhorse with a heavy steel prow.

"That damned boat's going to ram us!" shouted the pilot.

He rang for reverse, but no one had removed the bow-line from the trap. The line snapped tight and held them there as the prop rocked the boat impotently.

The tender was only forty or fifty yards away now, still full speed, aimed squarely amidships. Shooting dwindled to the single *whang* of the watchman's rifle. The fish pirate crew fled over the side, leaping to the water, to the trap timbers, keeping submerged or in shelter as they fought to get away.

Tim Calloway had issued the order that sent the tender directly for the pirate craft. Sunk there, at Cabbage Point, that seiner would be never-ending proof of the pirate's identity. There were four aboard — the engineer, Olaf, Jack Queens, and himself.

The engineer set the wheel and crawled aft, ready to go over the stern. Tim raised up to check their course. The tender was aimed dead amidships. At that moment he noticed a face at one of the ports — a woman's face — Eva Hartman!

He sprang toward the engine, hurling the prop to reverse. The sudden action threatened to strip gears and twist off the drive shafts, but the boat took it, bucking like a rodeo horse.

He swung the rudder. The boat skidded against her keel, sending a swell of water as large as she was. The combined actions broke her forward speed, but she went on side first and smashed against the pirate's hull with a crunch of steel plates.

Queens and Olaf were shouting at him, but Tim did not listen. He pulled himself up to the seiner's deck while she was still pitching. There was no one there to face him. He turned just as Tallant ran up from below.

Brynne Keefe had been knocked off balance by the impact. He regained his footing and nudged around the cabin with the Magnum revolver poised in his hand. He did not dare shoot because Tim and his son were too close together.

Jack Queens was climbing aboard. Keefe swung with the revolver. Queens saw it aimed at him for a fraction of a second. There was nothing he could do but release his hold and drop. The tender had been carried away, leaving him struggling in the water. Olaf tossed him a line.

Tallant Keefe tried to get away from Tim and locate his father, but the quarters were close there in the hatch. He was no good at rough and tumble, anyway.

"You coward!" Tallant sneered, picking himself up from the bottom of the hatch where Tim had flung him. "Send a woman to do your job for you!"

"What do you mean?"

"You know what I mean! And when the pater caught her, who was it saved her pretty skin? Me! I saved her!" Tallant spat blood from his bruised mouth and backed toward the engine room. When he was a few feet away, he turned suddenly and ran inside, clanking shut the metal fire door behind him.

"Eva!" Tim called.

He heard her answer through a bullet-riddled door right by his shoulder. The bolt grated, and it swung open. Eva was there, facing him, a small-caliber revolver still in her hand. She dropped the gun and came to his arms. "Oh, Tim, you don't think . . . ?"

"Of course not, Eva. I know why you're here."

Judge Hartman came out, a trifle disheveled. "I have the facts on this piracy now! I have enough to send them to prison for the next hundred years!"

From somewhere Tim could hear his name being shouted.

"Tim . . . the hatch . . . look out for the hatch . . ."

It was Jack Queens.

Tim turned away from Eva and climbed the steps of the hatch. He paused before reaching the last of them.

There was comparative quiet. Only a few shouts from the far side of the trap. Gulls veered overhead. A fresh salt breeze lifted a lock of his hair. The inlet was covered by choppy reflections of the morning sun.

Then he noticed something else. A shadow. It extended along the unswabbed deck planking from beside the cabin. Something about it was familiar. Brynne Keefe. Brynne Keefe with a gun.

Tim flipped out his own revolver — the double-action .45 he had been carrying that first night back in the Silver Salmon. Jack Queens had taken the gun away from him that night, but there was no choice now. He would have to shoot first or die.

He pointed the muzzle of the .45 against the hatch wall and pulled the trigger three times.

The gun rocked the narrow passage, filling it with choking powder smoke. Keefe muttered something, and his boots thumped the deck. Tim leaped to the

248

open, grabbed the casing of the hatchway, snapped himself around.

He expected Keefe to be retreating — if he had escaped those three bullets. He thought they would settle it with guns. But Keefe had not retreated. He had charged forward, and the two of them collided.

The unexpected impact knocked the gun from Tim's fingers. There was no chance to pick it up. Keefe was bringing the barrel of his Magnum into play.

Tim grabbed his wrist and thrust the gun high. It went off, and its heavy recoil knocked Keefe off balance for a second. Tim heaved him backward. They struck the cabin and were locked there in each other's strength.

Tim smiled through his teeth. "Afraid to face me without a pistol, Keefe?"

Keefe grunted. He sneered at the effrontery of this pup. Slowly, deliberately his fingers opened and the gun clomped to the deck.

"Satisfied?" he asked.

Tim nodded. He released his grip on Keefe's wrist and stepped back.

For that moment Tim's guard was too high. It was the advantage Keefe had wished. He sprang in, swinging his sledge-hammer fist with every ounce of his magnificent bulk. But unlike that evening back in the Silver Salmon, Tim was ready. He, too, had learned the tricks of the sailor's brawl. He used one of those tricks now. He took the punch with a swing of his body. At the second of its impact he came up with his left, jackknifed his arm short of its apex and closed it on Keefe's wrist.

For a second Keefe's fist was held in a vise formed by Tim's forearm and the muscles of his bicep. Keefe was not balanced correctly to jerk free. Tim wheeled back, carrying him farther off balance. Keefe lashed with his other fist, but he was in no position to put force in it, and, besides, Tim was bent over with only his shoulder and part of his head showing.

Then, with the speed of an uncoiling spring, Tim came up and around. The blow started with his toes and combined the strength of calves and thighs and back and the long, whiplash muscles of his arms. There was scarcely a sensation of it landing. It was that devastating. It knocked Keefe reeling. He struck the cabin, rebounded, hesitated in the middle of the deck. For the moment his eyes were blank as the eyes of a netted salmon.

Tim sprang forward, paused on the balls of his feet, and struck with a one-two left and right that made Keefe's head roll as though his neck were made of rubber. Tim took a massive haymaker that Keefe uncorked, shifted inside, and slammed him again. Keefe reeled backward, balanced momentarily on the rail, and fell overboard. He lashed around in the water between the seiner and the trap. His groping fingers located the trap timber, and he pulled himself up on it.

Tim was momentarily conscious of Olaf and Queens watching from the cockpit of the tender — of the Blue Star pirates on the timbers at the far side. It was truce for all hands while these giants of the canneries fought.

250

Tim sprang down just as Keefe pulled himself to one knee. He crouched, shaking water from his hair. He rose and timed a punch as Tim came in, but the old steam was gone. Tim took it, and kept coming, smashing him back.

Keefe fell half in the water. He made it up, some instinct keeping him on the eighteen-inch floating beam. Tim advanced, and Keefe wailed as he retreated along the timber.

"You've beaten me. You've smashed my business. What more do you want?"

It did not sound like Keefe. The sniveling words did not match the gleam in his eyes, either. He went to one knee as though to catch himself, and, as he did so, his hand reached back and closed on a wrecking bar. It was a heavy steel bar with a sharp, hooked end and two prongs for pulling spikes.

Keefe suddenly laughed and sprang up, the bar lifted high. But Tim came straight in. The heavy, hooked end missed, and only the shank found its mark. Tim's weight was unexpected. It rammed Keefe backward. Keefe clutched the bar to him and reeled back, trying to hold his slippery footing. He did not notice the end of the timber. Below him was the net-filled tunnel of the trap — that narrow, webbed opening below water where salmon were herded from the lead to the inner hearts.

He balanced a second, and plunged backward. He sank, lashing like a speared salmon, the hooked end of the big bar tangled in his gray sweater. He was down

251

there, fifteen feet below the surface, with the netting wrapped around him.

Tim stared at him, trying to shake the drug of battle from his brain. He seemed to come out of it suddenly. He reached for the nettings, trying to pull them, but they were tied fast.

The Blue Star pirates were over there, edged as close to the shore as they could get.

"Come here! Quick!" He was trying to drag the netting out, but it only tore the skin from his fingers. "We have to raise these tunnel nettings!"

The pirates did not move to save their vanquished leader. They were the rats who deserted their ship in the storm.

Tim yelled to Queens. The tender eased over against the trap, and Jack Queens and Olaf went to work raising the tangled netting. Tim opened a clasp knife and dove deeply, but it was useless, trying to cut through the many strands of tough webbing. Useless, and too late . . .

The noon sunshine was bright on the water when Big Chris showed up dressed only in his salvaged trousers, steering the government launch. He'd concealed himself in the evergreens until the pirate boat was gone, and then swam back after it.

"Aye bane geude feller from har on," he said piously to Tim and Eva as he pointed the boat toward Ketchanka. "Aye yust bane goin' to be honest fisherman, you bet. You don't want geude, strong feller at Gallway?"

"We might be able to use one," Tim said.

"Aye bane geude man in fight, too. Maybe Aye skal hunt up that Holgar The Horse and beat the yumpin yiminy right out of him, yah."

The judge spoke up: "Maybe you will need a fighter or two, my boy. I have it on good authority that the California Bank of I and C was going to take over Blue Star if Keefe failed. Those bankers will be tough competition for next year's run."

"Why, that will be fine." Tim grinned, standing comfortably close to Eva. "The tougher the better!"

About the Author

Dan Cushman was born in Osceola, Michigan, and grew up on the Cree Indian Reservation in Montana. He graduated from the University of Montana with a Bachelor of Science degree in 1934 and pursued a career in mining as a prospector, assayer, and geologist before turning to journalism. In the early 1940s his novelette-length stories began appearing regularly in such Fiction House magazines as *North-West Romances* and *Frontier Stories*. Later in the decade his North-Western and Western stories as well as fiction set in the Far East and Africa began appearing in *Action Stories*, *Adventure*, and *Short Stories*. *Stay Away, Joe*, which first appeared in 1953, is an amusing novel about the mixture, and occasional collision, of Indian culture and Anglo-American culture among the Métis (French Indians) living on a reservation in Montana. The novel became a bestseller and remains a classic to this day, greatly loved especially by Indian peoples for its truthfulness and humor. Yet, while humor became Cushman's hallmark in such later novels as *The Old Copper Collar* (1957) and *Good Bye, Old Dry* (1959), he also produced significant historical fiction in *The*

Silver Mountain (1957), concerned with the mining and politics of silver in Montana in the 1890s. This novel won a Spur Award from the Western Writers of America. His fiction remains notable for its breadth, ranging all the way from a story of the cattle frontier in *Tall Wyoming* (1957) to a poignant and memorable portrait of small-town life in Michigan just before the Great War in *The Grand and the Glorious* (1963).